George Rogers

Adventures of Elder Triptolemus Tub

Comprising important and startling Disclosures concerning Hell

George Rogers

Adventures of Elder Triptolemus Tub
Comprising important and startling Disclosures concerning Hell

ISBN/EAN: 9783337138806

Printed in Europe, USA, Canada, Australia, Japan

Cover: Foto ©Andreas Hilbeck / pixelio.de

More available books at **www.hansebooks.com**

ADVENTURES

OF

ELDER TRIPTOLEMUS TUB;

COMPRISING

IMPORTANT AND STARTLING DISCLOSURES

CONCERNING HELL;

ITS MAGNITUDE, MORALS, EMPLOYMENTS, CLIMATE, &C

ALL VERY SATISFACTORILY AUTHENTICATED.

TO WHICH IS ADDED,

THE OLD MAN OF THE HILL-SIDE.

———

BOSTON:

THE UNIVERSALIST PUBLISHING HOUSE,

No 37 CORNHILL.

1867.

CONTENTS.

1*

ADVENTURES

OF

ELDER TRIPTOLEMUS TUB

CHAPTER I.

In which the reader hath the honor of an introduction to Mr.
Tub, and is made acquainted with the scene of his very
marvellous adventures.

IF it shall ever be the reader's hap to fall
in with a personage exactly five feet high,
in his shoes; whose weight shall be exactly
two hundred and forty, avoirdupois; and
whose shadow on a wall shall reach to
exactly half the altitude when he lies on
his back as when he stands on his feet: if,
as to variety of hue, the nose of that same
individual shall resemble a conglomerate
specimen of mineralogy; if his upper and
nether person shall be encased in garments
of snuff-brown dye; and if, in the peculiar
twinkle of his eye, in his posture—inclining

out of plumb by a direction backward—in the self-complacent air with which he shall tap his polished boots with his walking-cane—in his whole bearing, in short, shall be exhibited a most comfortable persuasion of his own importance: why then, reader, I would wager great odds that you shall have had the ho r of falling in with my most respectable friend, Triptolemus Tub.

None other, reader, depend upon it, for nature never made *two* Triptolemus Tubs, of precisely the same length, breadth, and thickness : she never inflated another mass of corporiety with precisely the same quantum of the gas of self-esteem, nor encased she ever another conscience in so invulnerable a pericardium of obtusity. No, I am a believer in nature's omnipotence in everything but the making of two Triptolemus Tubs, and therefore, reader, shouldst thou chance to meet with the personage described, "put off the shoes from off thy feet," for he will be bound to be the veritable Triptolemus himself and none other.

Mr. Tub lives on the Virginian shore of

the Ohio river, a dozen miles or so below Wheeling; his dwelling is a massive one, of stone, two stories in height, and dingy from the smoke of bituminous coal, which is the chief fuel of that region; after the fashion which prevails thereabout, it has a passage through the centre from front to rear, and is destitute of the embellishment of frieze, or cornice, or even a porch, except we concede that respectable appellation to a platform projected before the front entrance, and flanked with a bench on each side. Good faith, it *bears* that appellation whether we concede it or not, and architecture among rustics must submit to just such names as they please to give it.

I will not assert that there is anything particularly pretty or romantic in the situation of the elder's domicile—for Mr. Tub, be it reverently kept in mind, *is* an elder— nothing less—except there be prettiness or romance in a straight reach of river with naked banks, a straight line of post-and- rail fence, and a straight unshaded road between. Little, however, cares our re- spectable acquaintance, Mr. Tub, about the

mere poetry of such matters.   What chiefly
engages his concern is a broad belt of rich
alluvial formation between the river and the
upland slopes, which to his matter-of-fact
mind suggests ideas of tall corn and fat
swine, something more substantial, I trow,.
than architectural gewgaws, or scene-struck
sentimentalities.

There is, nevertheless, an object near at
hand which well deserves a passing notice.
Near the large and naked trunk of an old
elm that leans over the water, and whose
roots, on the side next the river, are washed
bare by the attrition of the current, an ob-
long stone set into the ground, and project-
ing some three feet above it, is found to bear
the following rudely chiselled inscription :

SACRED

to the memory of twenty-six gallant men,
who fell on this spot in defence of the
women and children of the early settlement,
against a numerous party of Indians,
on the night of the 9th of June,
A. D. 1784.

Here, if the old elm were still in the pride
of its foliage, the traveller might be well

content to stop under its shadow, and rekindle the embers of his patriotism with the memories of bygone days; the trials and dangers encountered by the adventurous pioneers of the western wilderness. No life of courtly dalliance was theirs—not theirs the feebleness of body and mind resulting from luxurious sloth. The policy of insurance upon each man's life consisted of his customs, his sinews, his trusty rifle, and his hunting blade.

Our hero himself is not indifferent to the associations of this hallowed spot; on the contrary, the interests thereof are said to make their way to his heart through the plaits of fat in which it is so thickly encased; and this may well be believed, since among the band of heroes thus epitaphed repose the ashes of his father, Epaphroditus Tub.

Our friend Tub keeps a store and tavern convenient to the public road, where, reader, he will at any time be happy to see and serve you, on terms as honest as times will allow. I insert this advertisement for him gratis, for he is a very pious man, is elder

Tub, *very*, and—ahem! moderately honest, too, as times go. At all events, if he ever overcharges, or is beguiled by the temptations of the devil into frauds of any kind, he repents of it afterwards, or *means to* before he dies——and what more can piety require of any man?

Perhaps, for no human being is wholly exempt from failings, perhaps, I say, Mr. Tub may have slightly erred in the following important particular. There is a maxim in hackneyed use which advises, " Get along *honestly* in life if you can—if you cannot *honestly*, get along *anyhow*." Now it chanced to comport best with Elder Tub's notions of prudence to take this precept the tail-end foremost—he tried the *anyhow* first, and judged that when he should get rich at that, he could then better afford to practise honesty afterward.

There is *spiritual* economy, too, in this arrangement, he thought, for, in after life, when preparing for heaven by a repentance of past misdeeds, it will be found easier resisting the devil with a full pocket than with an empty one, and easier obtaining clerical assistance into the bargain. How ever that may be, the reader is earnestly advised not to make the experiment, since, amongst the numerous inconveniences by which the *anyhow* course is attended, not the least is that habits are thereby formed which it will task all the prudence and piety of after years to overcome. Let, then, HONESTY, FIRST, LAST, AND MIDST, be the reader's motto and governing principle through life.

Even the godly Mr. Tub has sore experience of the evil arising from long practice on the *anyhow* principle; a sore straining of his conscience does he find it to do, in any instance, the exactly honest thing. How, then, ought the godless, who have not the advantage of having been born again, as has elder Tub, take warning from his sad example.

But this, mind you, reader, is not to be construed as implying anything to the disparagement of Mr. Tub's character *God-ward*—by no manner of means—his *piety* still remains immaculate. If other evidence of that were wanting, this would suffice viz., that the church retains him amongst her most honored members, and——

But here, again, I am reminded that on this head the tongue of scandal has busied itself—as on what head will it not? In sooth it is the peculiar fate of saintship to be scandalized. For example, it has been insinuated that the elder would long since have been excommunicated but for his long purse, the scarcity of wealthy members, the usefulness of his daughter Keziah in distributing tracts, and begging pious charities, etc. But this, of course, is all sheer slander, and but illustrates the holy text, that "they who will live godly in Christ Jesus must suffer persecution." Nor is that same slander credible for another reason. Churches, everybody knows, are composed of godly persons; consequently, they are more tenderly considerate of their poor members than of their rich ones, and the pastors of the same—being more godly still —do much oftener visit and pay their courtesy to the poor than to the rich—of course they do.

Now, although it is confessed that an

ominous cloud now and then ariseth on the fair sky of Mr. Tub's reputation; and, although, moreover, the church hath several times called him to account therefor; and although, furthermore, he hath on each such occasion consented to increase his subscription for the minister, and the pious Keziah hath evinced an increase of zeal in her begging and tract dispensing charities; does it follow that the aforesaid scandalous insinuation hath in it any color of truth? By no manner of means. Most clearly not.

One thing, at all events, seems indubitably to be settled in regard to Mr. Tub, viz., that whatever may be the number of his *manward* obliquities, his *Godward* condition is unimpeachable. And he has, besides, one all-redeeming quality—one which, of itself, " will cover the multitude of sins," viz., he is most orthodox in faith, and particularly in respect to the article of endless damnation. " His *own* damnation?" Oh, by no means, dear simple reader, not his own; none but fools, or very nervous people, believe in their *own* damnation.

However, everybody is sure that *somebody*

will be damned, and *ought* to be, and Mr.
Tub is of everybody's opinion in that particular. But, then, as he is not to be included
among those who are to be damned, he very
properly gives himself no uneasiness about
the matter, but takes it as comfortably as
may be. It does not in the slightest degree
tend to check his tendency to corpulence.
He even goes to sleep, it is said, when his
pastor, the Rev. Mr. Smearsoul, comes to
that part of his sermon in which that edifying item is descanted upon. And why
should he not? seeing that neither to himself, nor his kith, nor kin, it can have the
remotest applicability. His experience in
relation thereto is summed up in the following luscious verses :—

" Praised be the Lord, I pardoned am,
   My spouse, good soul, is pardoned too,
We shall be saved, through Christ the Lamb,
   In spite of all that we can do.

Our children, six in number, all
   (By pious parents sanctified,)
Are safe in grace whate'er befall,
   For who shall Christ's elect divide ?

For others, it is nought to me
  Who shall be saved, or who be damned,
For grace shall still exalted be,
  And saints rejoice tho' hell be crammed."

    2*

CHAPTER II.

Elder Tub ruminateth. An apparition of doubtful charac ter introduceth himself. He describeth hell as being a far more tolerable place than it is generally believed to be ; and giveth a pleasing and very probable account of its good state of society.

ELDER TUB sat at the foot of the old elm one moonlight evening, ruminating on the trials and dangers which were encountered in life by the brave men whose fate was registered on the rude stone near him; an unwonted sensibility stole over his heart on the occasion, insomuch that it wholly abstracted his attention from surrounding objects. "Noble fellows!" exclaimed he, "thus to have torn yourselves from the attractions of civilized life, and to have ventured forth into this then howling wilderness, inhabited only by savages and wild varmints. How much our now smiling and populous country owes to your exertions and sacrifices! Yet here you lie, with

nothing but this rock to tell that you ever lived, or in what cause you died. Well, rest in peace, brave hearts! for if our coun-. try is thus ·unmindful of her benefactors, thar's mighty·comfort in knowing that heaven——"

Our soliloquist was here interrupted by sounds which resembled a suppressed gig-gle—" He, he, he!" ·

His first impression was that they pro-ceeded from one of his negroes—of which he owned a score or so—and feeling both his piety and his patriotism to be insulted by such ill-timed merriment, he clutched his cane with the meek purpose of knock-ing the offender down; but—horror of hor-rors, with what a vision was he greeted! Was it human, or was it spirit? It seemed too shadowy for the one—too corporeal for the other. Over its deep-set eyes, in which twinkled a world of cunning humor, beetled a pair of shaggy brows, from which the forehead sloped back in a fashion that no phrenologist would like, inasmuch as it indicated anything but a good moral development.   Poor Tub felt his hat to rise involuntarily from his head,

> " And each particular hair to stand on end,
>   Like quills upon the fretful porcupine."

The apparition continued to regard him with humorous interest for some moments, sitting much at its ease, within a few yards of him, and peering at him with its twinkling optics as if it would look him through.

"Mr. Tub," it said at length, "don't be alarmed at my sudden appearance here, nor take offence at my seeming rudeness in breaking in upon your soliloquy.   I meant no contempt for the sentiments you uttered, Mr. Tub; but your closing remark—or, rather, the remark with which you were *about* to close—was so unorthodox, that, coming from you, an elder of the church, it betrayed me out of my usual gravity for the moment.   *He, he!* it really *was* a laughable mistake in you, my good friend, to suppose that patriotism, or any other merely *moral* virtue, is held in any sort of esteem in heaven!   Why, know you not that all its favors are lavished on those who have been born again? And this, you must know, is a degree in religious experience which is seldom taken by brave men who die for their country, and most assuredly was not by a single one of those on whose fate you were ruminating. I say this from certain knowledge, Mr. Tub, for my own bones—— Nay, don't start, my friend—you are perfectly safe in my company—my own bones lie beneath that stone; and my spiritual abode is—where all theirs is whose fate is recorded on that rude tablet—where that of forty-nine fiftieths is, who are sent to eternity from the battle-field——*It is in the world of woe*, Mr. Tub."

A deep pause of some moments here ensued, during which the elder was struggling between his fears and his curiosity; at length the apparition resumed his discourse in the same familiar strain.

"My name, on earth, Mr. Tub, was Shadrach Paddle, and I passed for a tolerably honest and clever fellow, I believe; I was on terms of great intimacy with Epaphroditus Tub, your father; together we fought and fell at last, on this very spot,

and we found ourselves in hell together at
the same moment of time. Your mother,
and my wife, Dolly Paddle—who never did
any harm in her life, poor soul, but that of
neglecting to be born again—and the rest
of the women who were tomahawked on
the occasion, had arrived there about an
hour before us, and were taking on sadly at
their hard fortune, poor creatures, especially at their being separated from their children, who, however, it was a consolation
to them to know, had gone to a happier
world——

"You shake your head, Mr. Tub," continued the goblin, "and I know what thought
is passing through your mind at this moment,
—you think that the relations of one with
another in time are all forgotten in eternity.
So your divines persuade you, and doubtless they have their motive therefor. They
would find it hard, for instance, to keep the
saints in comfort, in reference to their own
parents, partners, children, who died without due preparation for heaven, except they
could persuade them that in the spirit-life
all these ties pass from remembrance for-

ever. How, then, do these divines dispose of the case of the rich man, in the parable? Did not he know Abraham? Did not Abraham still recognize him as his son? Was he not still concerned for the welfare of his five brethren? Ah, friend Tub, that device for quieting the plea of the affections in behalf of kindred damned, will not do; your priests, Mr. Tub, must devise something more feasible, and better authenticated.

"Well, to resume my narrative: it was not long after our arrival in hell ere we all became pretty well reconciled to the country, hot as it is; more especially as we found there nearly all our brave countrymen who, some ten years before, had been sent thither from the bloody fields of Lexington and Bunker Hill; and others of later arrival from Monmouth, Saratoga, Trenton, and other revolutionary battle-grounds. These brave fellows, I was pleased to learn, had become pretty well inured to the climate, and could now endure its discomforts with tolerable composure. Custom, you

3

know, Mr. Tub, will reconcile us to anything.

"And, take my word for it, my friend,
the society of hell—bating that it has no
religion—is far more respectable than mortals are aware of. You must be convinced
of this when you consider of what distinguished personages a large portion of it is
composed. By far the most of your revolutionary heroes are there, Mr. Tub; those
who commanded your armies and ships;
who signed the declaration of your inde-
pendence; who thundered against tyranny
in your legislative halls; who presided in
your national councils, and even occupied
your chief executive chair; whose deeds,
moreover, are the theme of history and
of song; but who neglected, nevertheless, to
get religion, and to shape their opinions
thereof by a creed, and are therefore, de-
spite their moral and patriotic virtues, consigned to the realms of hell forever.

"For it is the essence of orthodoxy, Mr.
Tub—as you, an elder of the church, must
be aware—that virtue, and patriotism, are
but filthy rags in the estimation of Heaven,

unless those who exercise them shall happen to have been born again. Moreover, there is, as your own divines allow, *no change after death;* of course, then, these virtues continue to be exercised in hell, and the personages alluded to continue to be there distinguished by the excellent qualities which distinguished them on earth. Hence, Mr. Tub, there is a large aggregate of moral excellence in hell.

"On the other hand, some very scurvy rascals have gone to heaven to my certain knowledge. There was Anthony Pimp, for instance, who deserted our colony with a dozen horses he had stolen, and who, to obliterate the evidence of his infamy, guided the Indians to our encampment at midnight, and thereby effected our destruction. I made sure of Anthony's arrival in hell when his term on earth should expire; I was equally certain that, except accident should befriend him, his term would be cut short by the hangman sooner or later. And it was, sure enough; but he managed his spiritual matters more shrewdly than I anticipated, for he got religion before he graced the gallows, and is now in heaven, singing psalms. *He, he!* Anthony will have found many a shrewd rogue in his new home, who defrauded the devil at the last pinch after the same fashion.

"In my simplicity, Mr. Tub, I looked about me in hell for a considerable time after my arrival there, in quest of certain persons of whom I had read in history, who had distinguished themselves by deeds of ferocity and persecution. I had read, for instance, of the founding of the Inquisition by St. Dominic—of the *Te Deum* performed by Pope Innocent, when the news reached him of the massacre of 40,000 Protestants on St. Bartholemew's day—of the burning of Servetus, by Calvin—of Cotton Mather's brutality at the hanging of Rev. George Burroughs, &c. 'Of a surety,' thought I, 'those canting persecutors are in hell for these dark deeds.' ·I was mistaken, nevertheless : their victims were mostly there, but their murderers had died in the odor of sanctity, and gone to the other country.

"Hence I learned that persecution, when the party committing it is Orthodox, and the victim a heretic, is not included in the catalogue of damning sins. O no, Mr. Tub, but few of those who imbrue their hands in the blood of heretics are doomed to an abode in our ungodly place, and this, also, is favorable to our good state of society.

"How often do you hear it said, Mr. Tub, that 'there ought to be a hell for *somebody.*' Granting there ought—do those same *somebodies* get to it? On the contrary, does it not oftener happen that the more moral and peaceable class of people neglect to be born again, whilst the profligate, the profane, the violent, make sudden work of the matter, and help largely to swell the company of the saints on earth and the saved in heaven? Even your own preachers will inform you, Mr. Tub, that there is a far slenderer chance of a moral man's salvation than that of an out-breaking villain's. Hence, you see that hell has every chance for a very decent state of society, and, on that score, for being a very decent and orderly sort of place."

Another pause here ensued; our friend Triptolemus was utterly astounded at the nature of these disclosures; their strange-

3*

ness; the familiar manner in which the goblin addressed him; his near concern in the
matters revealed, and the air of entire probability which the statements of Paddle
wore, quite overcame the elder's fears, and
emboldened him to hold converse with his
queer visitor. His poor old father and mother in hell! Alas! he had not before
dreamed of such a thing. Yet what more
possible? since, as he well knew, they were
destitute of that mysterious qualification
which is held to be essential to one's admission into heaven, although possessed of
many virtues which rendered them useful
and amiable on earth.

Such, also, was the case in general with
the hardy pioneers of the west: coarse in
manners and in speech; ignorant of, and
indifferent about, the mysteries of the
Christian faith; yet frank-hearted, hospita-
ble, and reckless of hardship and danger
when responding to the calls of duty and
humanity; their dying-beds were seldom
cheered by the voice of religion, or their
graves sanctified by its prayers.

"Am I, then, to believe, Mr. Paddle,"

the elder took courage to inquire, "that you are really an inhabitant of the lower pit, and that my parents—the whole twenty-six who lie under this rock—and the women of the settlement who were massacred on that fearful night, are all now included amongst he damned?"

"No preaching was ever more true, Mr. Tub, whether you believe it or not," was Paddle's reply. "If you credit these statements, well; and if not, well; it is a rule in the divine government, it seems, to burn people for their want of faith, and the same has been extensively adopted in the practice of godly men on earth—as witness the fires of Smithfield and the Inquisition—but opinion in hell is free.

"I don't wonder at its being unpalatable truth to you that so many of those are in hell who achieved your national liberties; I know it would not sound well in a fourth-of-July oration; full oft have I been invisibly present on such days, and laughed in the orator's face as he was descanting on the virtues of those brave men, and pointed to heaven as the place where they are receiving the meed of their servᵢₑ· *he!* And your divines, Mr. Tub, dare not offend the patriotism of the people by hinting that these same heroes may possibly be in a very different country.

"Now is it likely, Mr. Tub, that amidst the bustle, and heat, and passion, which revolutionary times and conflicts are apt to excite, those gallant fellows took leisure to concern themselves about faith and the new birth? Not much did old Putnam, I trow, nor Warren, nor Greene, nor Moultrie, nor De Kalb, nor Paul Jones. And, to come to later times, who suspects that Decatur, or Lawrence, or Jefferson, or Franklin, with many others whom I could name, were subjects of regeneration and an evangelical faith? It has been asserted of even the great Washington, that although he gave a general assent to the truth of Christianity, he stopt widely short of an evangelical conversion.

"Of course I could tell you exactly how that matter stands, but I spare your patriotic feelings. Be assured, however, that hell contains a very large majority of the most learned and illustrious men that have existed on earth—poets, orators, statesmen, priests, historians, sages, and monarchs; and whilst the wise maxims and precepts of some of these form the elements of the moral code for millions of mankind, they themselves are in hell because, in addition to their good morality, they did not also get religion—a thing they might have got very cheaply, and (as in the case of the thief on the cross) at their very last extremity."——"But, Mr. Paddle," broke in the elder ——"Not a word, Mr. Tub," interrupted Paddle in return; "I divine what you are about to say, my friend, and will save you the discredit of uttering a sentiment so unorthodox. Remember, Mr. Tub, that you are an *elder*, and ought, therefore, to be sound in the faith. Now you were about to suggest that possibly some of these very respectable persons are admitted to heaven, even without having been evangelically regenerated, on the score of their rare *moral* excellencies.

"My friend, the thing is not to be thought of—it is decidedly heretical. So taught not

Bunyan, nor Hervey, nor Toplady, nor Doddridge, nor Gill, nor Scott, nor Owen, nor, indeed, any of the class of divines termed evangelical. Not even Arminians so teach—though with *their* creed it would better consist than with Calvinism.

"For example, on the parable of the rich man and Lazarus, Archbishop Usher, and after him Adam Clarke, (we are wondrous book-wise in hell, Mr. Tub,) asserts that Christ prefers no charge whatever against the rich man's moral character— that, on the contrary, he may have been a very upright and charitable gentleman, and only lacked the one thing needful, or a sound conversion, to qualify him for an abode among the blessed. Of course, then, as persons may possess a great deal of amiability and yet be damned, it is clear that hell must contain a large amount of most delectable society——But," exclaimed Paddle, with some alarm, "the moon, I see, is getting high above the hills; I must therefore be gone, Mr. Tub, for my person don't show to advantage in a strong light, and the light of the sun is still more prejudicial thereto than moonshine. I will see you again and renew these topics, Mr. Tub. Farewell."

In another moment Shadrach Paddle was gone—not a trace of him was left; the elder rubbed his eyes, and strained his vision to the utmost, but to no effect, save that he did fancy that he saw a streak of mist ascending the mountain-side. He could not on oath affirm it to have been Paddle, however, nor any relation of his; neither can I. The elder began to be doubtful at length whether his eyes and ears might not have been all the while deceiving him, and whether the whole matter of the supposed interview might not have been a trick of the imagination. Perhaps it was; the reader can decide as to that as well as I; I give it to him as I got it.

CHAPTER III.

OUR friend Triptolemus could not summon courage enough, on the next evening, to await his visitant's visit at the foot of the elm tree, but he sat out on one of the benches of the porch afore described, and as he smoked his pipe, and watched the alternate play of moonlight and shadow on the placid river, he ruminated with huge profundity on the matters of Paddle's communication.

"No, it's clar against possibility," muttered he at length, as he knocked the ashes out of his pipe; "to think of people's ever getting used to hell-fire is mighty unreasonable; a salamander itself could not stand it; why, Parson Smearsoul says that the

intensest heat of a lime-kiln is ice itself
compared with hell's temperature, and that
the same will grow hotter and hotter to all
eternity. So its clar out of reason to think
of ever getting used to it. And, besides—as
Parson Smearsoul also says—it aint literal
fire after all; 'fire,' he says, 'is only used as
a figure; the real suffering of the damned
is from remorse.' These are his very words,
and all our best commentators confirm that
opinion. So that point is settled.

"Well, as to the society of the place. I
am willing to admit that a great many
respectable people are sent to hell one time
and another, and it really is true, as Paddle
says, that moral folk are in much greater
danger of being damned than are outbreak-
ing sinners, 'because,' to quote Parson
Smearsoul again, 'the latter can be fright-
ened, and thus brought to repentance, while
the former feel safe on the ground of their
own uprightness. Conscience, tharfore,
fails to alarm the moral man, and he is not
undeceived as to the worthlessness of his
morality until he finds himself in hell.' So
says Parson Smearsoul, and I conclude,

4

tharfore, that it's best for a man to sin with a whole hand while he is about it, and not merely half do the thing.

" However, altho' so many of hell's inhabitants may be decent folk when they go thar, yet they soon change for the worse. That's certain.   The doctrine of *no change after death*, means that people can't change for the better—but they may for the worse for all that.   Indeed it's a clar case, for I have heard the Reverend Mr. Smearsoul say so.   'The damned,' says he, ' get worse and worse to all eternity.'   So I've got back to the true point of faith again, thank God."

As the elder arrived at this self-satisfying conclusion he happened to turn his eyes toward the other side of the porch, and there, to his astonishment, sat Mr. Shadrach Paddle very much at his ease, and waiting, apparently, with great politeness, until the thread of our hero's reasoning should run out; this point arrived at he gave vent to one of his quiet laughs—*he, he!*—and then addressed the elder as follows.

"I plainly perceive, Mr. Tub, that you

are no philosopher; nor need you regret that, since the being a fool considerably increases one's chance of being saved at last. I myself went to hell with no large stock of sense; but one cannot be long there without greatly increasing his capital of information. Frequent intercourse with the numerous gifted intellects comprised in hell's community tends to diffuse a high degree of intelligence through the entire mass. All the heathen philosophers are with us, Mr. Tub, besides innumerable wits, poets, logicians, statesmen, and literati from Christendom: one must be a dull scholar not to improve in such society.

"We have blind Homer, the father of song; Virgil, his most gifted disciple; Horace, Ovid, Euripides, Juvenal, Pindar—in short all the bards of antiquity, and nearly all of modern times, especially such as profaned their gifts by writing for the stage. Of course Shakspeare is with us; and Butler, (or Hudibras,) and Dryden, and Pope, and Ben Jonson, and Otway, and Collins, and Cowley, and Rowe, and Swift, besides thousands of different nations whose names you would not recognize. Their misfortune was to be seeking for words that would conform to rhyme and metre when they should have been seeking to save their souls.

"Then we also have historians; as Herodotus, Xenophon, Tacitus, Livy, Sallust, Plutarch, Suetonius. Also of modern times, as Gibbon, Hume, Bolingbroke, Clarendon, Smollet, and others. Of sages, both heathen and Christian, we have an ample complement; as Socrates, Pythagoras, Plato, Aristotle, Zeno, Diogenes, the two Catoes; besides the moderns, Spinosa, Rousseau, Voltaire, Franklin, and so on.

"Need I name statesmen, orators, physicians, warriors, and men of science? We have Cicero, Demosthenes, the two Brutuses, Themistocles, Alcibiades, Strabo, the two Plinys, Esculapius, Hippocrates, in short, too many to be particularized. *So* many, indeed, and constituting, whether we regard their talents or their virtues, so brilliant an assembly, that the benevolence of people begins to be startled in these times at the idea of peopling hell with such decent company, and the good orthodox faith is

much endangered by recent attempts to
have it otherwise.

"It is asserted, for instance, that men
may get to heaven without believing in
Christ, or being born again, provided that
they have not had the gospel preached to
them, and have lived pretty decently without it.   Now if this were so, Mr. Tub, why
should missionaries be sent to preach to the
heathen—especially as it costs so much?
It may be doubted whether more do not live
moral lives *without* the gospel, than attain a
miraculous change of heart *with* it.   Why
then, I repeat, since, without it, the terms
of salvation are easier, should men be paid
for preaching the gospel to the heathen,
which increases the difficulty of the terms
of salvation, and lessons their chance of
getting to heaven at last?

"Poor economy, methinks, Mr. Tub, especially as the having heard the gospel will
make hell the hotter to those who shall fail
of being converted by it.   *Poor economy*, I
repeat, Mr. Tub, *poor economy*, sir!   But,
then, you know, my friend, this notion of
the salvability of the heathen without the

4*

gospel is but a novelty of a later age, and is one of those lies which are saddening the hearts of the righteous who continue to believe in the good old way.

"And now, elder Tub, I will set you right in regard to the points you were reasoning with yourself upon when I took my seat here. And first. You think it improbable that people can become inured to hell's temperature, so that, at length, it shall cease to be disagreeable to them.

"You must know, Mr. Tub, that heat and cold are but relative circumstances. Look yonder at the planet Mercury, whose orbit is scores of millions of miles nearer the sun than is that of your earth, and its climate is such that, were your vast oceans removed thither, they would almost instantly be converted into vapor, and a mortal who should be translated thither would soon be scorched to a cinder. Yet it is a peopled world, Mr. Tub, and its inhabitants are as well pleased with its temperature as you are with this of yours. When their astronomers survey this earth, it makes them shiver to think of beings living in so frozen a clime as they pronounce this to be, even within the equatorial circle.

"Now, with regard to hell, our constitutions are fitted to endure its heat, or they are not; if they are, long use will not fail to reconcile us to it; if they are not, we must of necessity waste under its influence, (for *pain* implies *waste*,) and annihilation must at length ensue. Your shrewd divines would seem to have become aware of this fact; hence some of them have substituted the doctrine of annihilation for that of endless torture; while others would persuade you that hell-fire is but a metaphor, and that the real punishment of the damned consists of remorse. Now, that remorse it *cannot* be, I will most satisfactorily prove to you.

"It is absolutely essential to the existence of remorse that the *moral feelings* should be active; and as these become torpid remorse ceases. Hence it is, that the more pious the individual is, the keener is his remorse for the slightest deviation from duty. Hence, too, as an individual progresses in crime his moral sensibilities become blunted, and remorse in him becomes less keen and less frequent. Now, your divines say that the damned are *wholly* lost to goodness, and *wholly* filled with wickedness. That being true, Mr. Tub, how *can* they be exercised with the slightest possible degree of remorse? The thing is impossible.

"But remorse cannot take place in hell for another reason. We never can remorsefully regret having sinned against a being we hate—whilst hate is active, remorse, in relation to the same being, never can be. On the contrary, in proportion to our love for a being, will be our remorse for having sinned against him. If we even do not really *love* him, yet, if we are conscious of his claims upon our *gratitude*, on the ground of benefits conferred, we still will be remorseful for having violated so many and obvious obligations, and will regret that some peculiarities in the individual prevent the possibility of our loving him. Now, is it likely that God is loved in hell, Mr. Tub? Is it even likely that the damned can regard nim as their benefactor, in having imposed on them an existence which he clearly foresaw would prove to them a ceaseless curse ? Of course not, and remorse in hell therefore is clearly impossible.

" You mortals charge your ruin upon the Devil, but we in hell know that the Devil has no power but what the Creator gave him, and that he who, having created children in his own image, let loose upon them a host of malignant spirits who coveted their destruction, is at least as responsible for the foreseen disastrous result, as they can be who were instrumental in effecting it. It is thus *we* reason, Mr. Tub, and we therefore fail to see any obligations of gratitude to be due from us to God; on *no* ground, therefore, is remorse in hell a possibility.

"Thus far I have reasoned on your own premises; but as to our growing worse and worse in hell, let us look into that. In hell we have no fleshly appetites to gratify, and they, with mortals, are the primary source of sin; we have no gold to excite avarice; no food nor drink to induce intemperance; no distinctions of sex to excite lust, that most prolific cause of mischief among men. Gambling cannot be practised in hell, seeing

that nothing can be there lost nor won.
Nor, where there are no dominions to be
conquered, can ambition take place, nor its
concomitant, war.   An illicit amour with
a beautiful woman led to the siege and
destruction of Troy; but hell can give birth
to no such circumstance.   The bard Milton
seems to have appreciated hell's advantage
over earth in this respect; hence he ex-
claims,

" 'O, shame to man—devil with devil damned
    Firm concord keeps; men only disagree
    Of creatures rational.'

"On earth, too, millions have sadly
groaned in dungeons, on racks, and in
flames, to glut the hungry maw of super-
stition; but in hell we have no religion to
incite us to persecute one another. How,
then, *can* we grow worse and worse?

"No being, Mr. Tub, ever sinned for
mere sinning's sake; but for what could be
gained by it, and as in hell *nothing* can be
gained thereby, so in hell there can be no
motive for sinning. I know well that your
divines are wont to affirm that the source
and motive of all wickedness is *hatred of*

God. But this is sheer nonsense. If a man gets drunk, for instance, is it *hatred of God* which induces him to it, or *love of rum?* The latter, undoubtedly. So if a man abuses his neighbor, it is hatred of, or anger toward his neighbor, which actuates him, not hatred of God. Men are ambitious, through a love of power or conquest—they are libertines through a love of sensual gratification; and so on, but as to God, they never take a thought how their conduct is to affect him. Man is, by a law of his nature, a selfish being, and acts for self.

"So you see, my friend, that hell is a far more tolerable place, in every view of it, than it is generally believed to be; and we have one undeniable advantage over those who leave this earth for heaven, which I wish you to take into serious consideration. It very rarely happens, Mr. Tub, that a whole family gets to heaven, either together or separately; sometimes the wife gets there, whilst her husband and children are damned; sometimes a part of the children are saved, and find that neither father nor mother has attained the same desirable des-

tiny. They are, then, orphans in heaven.
Now as to hell, how often do whole families
—nay, whole communities—arrive thither
at the same moment of time! The whole
earth's population, for instance, at the time
of the flood, and the communities of Sodom
and Gomorrah at the time of their destruction. Now this, Mr. Tub, is no inconsider-
able advantage which hell has over heaven,
for although the fleshly relations are dissolved at death, yet the relations of mind
with mind are not thus dissolved, nor can
they be."

"Why, really, Mr. Paddle!" exclaimed
the astonished Triptolemus, "you quite puz-
zle and confound me; I never thought of
matters in such a light before; I now see
thar's mighty little chance of your being so
bad in hell as you are represented. But
then, as you don't employ yourselves in
serving God as they do in heaven, I should
think that time would pass mighty heavily
with you for lack of something to beguile it
with."

"Not at all, Mr. Tub," replied the goblin; "not at all; we beguile it in numerous

pleasant ways. Being no longer encumbered with our mortal nature, the intellect is less clouded by passion and prejudice, and can therefore exercise its powers more freely. We have lessons on history from the old historians, and as the chief part of the heroes in the various wars therein mentioned are with us, they can furnish the details of the same, and correct the errors of the original accounts. For my own part I am fond of hearing our revolutionary battles described by those who fought and fell therein.

"Well, then we have new poems now and then, from Homer, Shakspeare, Voltaire, and others. Conceive, Mr. Tub, how grand must necessarily be these productions, when a Cæsar, a Hannibal, a Napoleon, recites his battles, and a Homer, or Virgil, or Byron, converts the history into song.

"Then we have philosophical lectures and experiments in great plenty; our own Franklin has made many new discoveries in electricity, which is a matter of much importance, for hell is considerably subject

5

to thunder-storms. Archimedes explains to us those wondrous contrivances, by which he so long baffled the Roman army when it besieged his native city of Syracuse. We have among us the architects of those vast structures which stand amidst the sandy wastes of Egypt and Ethiopia. Semiramis is with us, and Sesostris, as are also all the Pharaohs, as well as the Kings of Babylon, Nineveh, Thebes, Carthage, and other renowned ancient empires, whose ruins continue to be a study and a wonder to your antiquarians and *savans*. Hell, too, is an exceedingly favorable field for chemical experiments, and of these we have an abundance by Lavoisier, Priestley, and thousands of others. But time, Mr. Tub, would fail me for detailing the numerous devices by which our attention, in hell, is diverted from the uncomfortable heat of the climate.

"In all ages of the world, Mr. Tub, men of enlarged minds have found it difficult to conceive, how the Creator can justly hold his rational creatures accountable for their mistakes of opinion. Such, also, have usually been indifferent about attendance at church, and the memorizing of creeds; they have somehow taken it into their heads that the best service of the Creator consists in acts of beneficence to his creatures. Hence millions of men, who were excellent husbands and fathers; and millions of women, who were amiable wives and tender mothers; hence, too, millions of both sexes, who were intent through life on living usefully and beneficently for mankind, omitted to get religion, join a church, and save their immortal souls.

" Well, we prize highly in hell those virtues which heaven holds so cheap, and when we see a tithe of the good which results therefrom to the world effected by *evangelical conversion*, we shall prize that too; but at present—such is the dimness of our spiritual vision—we hold that same conversion about as cheaply as the saints hold the moral and social virtues—to be valued it must be spiritually discerned, no doubt.

" Well, thus it has happened, that myriads of the most brilliant and gifted of mortals have, by the deceptive light of philosophy, or the bewildering glare of genius, neglected to commit their creeds, and blundered down to the infernal pit. However, retaining still those social and moral virtues, (for there is *no change after death,*) they compose a most splendid and delectable society where they are, and the same goes far toward rendering hell a very tolerable place of abode."

A slight noise here called off the elder's attention for a moment, and on his resuming it Paddle was clean gone—not even a streak of mist was visible. "Can it be?" exclaimed the elder, in utter bewilderment. "Can my senses a second time have been deceiving me? Impossible; for I should never, of myself, have thought of matters so new, and startling. Heigh—o! Well, I must keep them to myself, or I shall be suspected of having talked these strange things to my own ear, and my orthodoxy will thus fall under suspicions." So concluding, the elder went in and took his seat near the kitchen fire by his spouse Dorothy Tub.

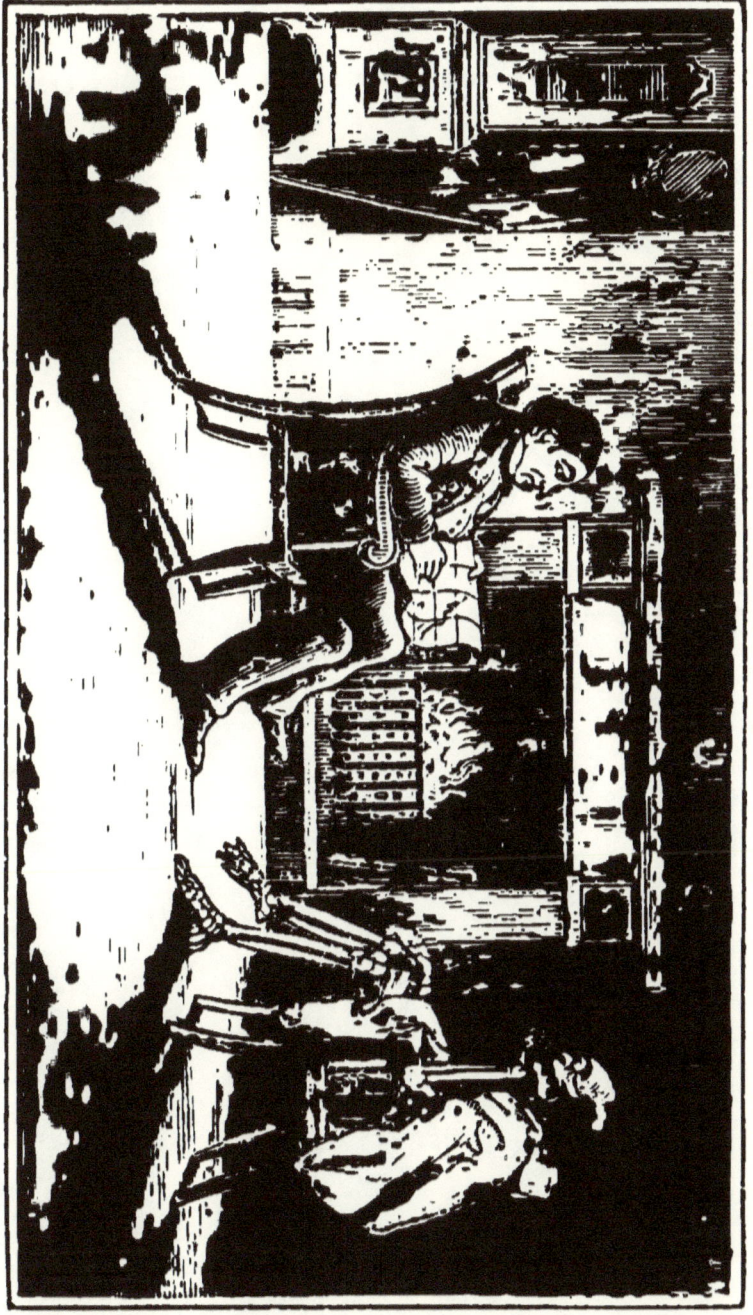

CHAPTER IV.

*The elder experienceth a huge expansion of ideas in regard
to the magnitude of the earth ; whereupon Paddle—finding Mr. Tub's ideas in a growing state—greatly addeth
to their enlargement by convincing him of the stupendous
dimensions of the lower world, and the numerousness of its
inhabitants.*

On the third night of our narrative elder
Tub would not trust himself out of doors,
for although Paddle had proved a harmless
visitant in his former interviews, yet the
elder felt an undefinable fear of him, and a
mistrust as to the purpose of his visits; he
therefore kept himself close in the chimney
corner, and was employed through most of
the evening in perusing a map of the globe.
The great magnitude of the earth had never
loomed so largely to his mental vision as it
then did, and he was utterly amazed as his
mind gradually expanded to a realization of
it. Ever and anon he muttered his astonishment to Dorothy Tub, who occupied

an arm-chair in the other chimney-corner, which was the match to the one that contained his own portly person.

"Really! Dorothy, my dear, this is a mighty big world of ours! The 'Old Dominion,' of itself, is a monstrous big piece of ground. Then thar's Pennsylvania—and Ohio—and New York—all the eastern—all the western—the middle, and southern states! Then thar's the country away across the rocky mountains to the Pacific—and the immense tract across our national limit to the north pole—and Texas and Mexico on the south! And after all, I have scarcely mentioned an eighth part of the solid portion of our globe, and scarcely two thirds of America alone! Only think, Dorothy Tub!"

·The elder looked up on making this last appeal to his spouse; but no Dorothy Tub was there to sympathize in his amazement —her arm-chair was vacant. Nor, in truth, had elder Tub any right to expect that Mrs. Tub would continue there to play echo to his exclamations, for she herself had employment in the same line, on the score of

certain corns and rheumatic affections,
which, by their peculiar uneasiness, prog-
nosticated a change in the weather. And
she had so declared through the evening
again and again; but Mr. Tub had been too
profoundly engaged to heed her complaints,
—and it thus happeneth oft with men, when
their wives are detailing their aches and
pains, and the same is a crying sin on their
part. As to Dorothy, when she had ascertained that Mr. Tub was deaf to her interesting recital, she vacated her chair, and
betook herself to bed in a huff.

"A monstrous big world," exclaimed the
elder, continuing his erudite cogitations,
"for besides Europe—and Asia—and Africa
—there are New Holland, and New South
Wales, besides numerous islands in the different oceans ; and, after all, full three
fourths of the globe are covered with water.
Why, I wonder"——

Here a significant "ahem!" from the opposite arm-chair, broke in upon his speculations, and on his looking in that direction, his
surprise was great at beholding Shadrach
Paddle therein seated, and regarding him

with the same expression of humorous interest as upon former occasions.

"You think your world a large one, Mr.
Tub," said that queer personage, "what
then would you think, could you appreciate
the magnitude of hell? Why, my friend, in
comparison therewith your globe is no bigger than a hazel-nut. The planet Jupiter
would make eight hundred such worlds as
yours; but hell would make *more* than that
many Jupiters—nay, it would make more
than all the globes in your planetary system, the sun included. This, at first thought,
may seem an extravagant statement, but
reflection, Mr. Tub, and estimating the fact
upon data admitted by your own creed, will
satisfy you that I am not far amiss. Let us
calculate.

"The population of your earth is vari-
ously computed at from eight to twelve
hundred millions. We will take ten hundred millions as a medium. This number
of human beings is swept into eternity and
renewed every twenty-five years, and for all
these heaven and hell are the only recep-
tacles.

‘ A heaven, a hell, and these alone,
Beyond the present life are known,
There is no middle state.’

So sang Watts, and Watts was orthodox.
Now, what proportion of all these does hell
receive? I will not require you to take the
true answer to this important question on
the mere statement of Shadrach Paddle—
although of his credibility I have a better
opinion than I have of most of your theo-
logical estimates on this subject—but you
shall have it, my friend, on the faith of fair
arithmetical computation.

"Of the ten hundred millions, then, who
people this globe, only two hundred millions
are comprised within Christendom; the residue is made up of Jews, Mahomedans and
Pagans. Of the number who are *nominally*
Christians, what proportion are *really* such?
How many, for instance, are *born again?*
—for without that qualification they are not
eligible to salvation. Is one in thirty thus
eligible, Mr. Tub? Think soberly, take all
Christendom—Catholic, Protestant, and
Greek—does one in thirty exhibit evidence

of being born again? Nay, not one in sixty even.

"Nevertheless, in consideration that all who die in infancy go to heaven, (and therefore is it a great piece of good luck thus to die,) I will admit that a thirty-second part of all Christendom is saved. Six millions and a fourth, out of two hundred millions! Which leaves for hell's quota, out of the whole *Christian* portion of mankind, the sum of one hundred and ninety-three millions and three fourths—every twenty-five years! At this rate alone, you see, Mr. Tub, hell is peopling much faster than any other country we hear of.

"Of the remaining eight hundred millions of earth's population, the most of Christians now think, and formerly *all* thought, that not *any* will be saved. We will take, nevertheless, the opinion of the minority on this head, viz. that salvation is possible to those heathens who improve to the utmost such scanty advantages as they possess. We will take this, I say, although there is much, and weighty orthodox authority against it. For example, looking the other night (for I don't go at large by day) over the shoulder of a pious old lady, who, with spectacles on nose, was reading Saurin's sermons, I saw that that French divine, although a Protestant, and reputed liberal, utterly scouts the modern notion that salvation is possible to the heathen.

"'Some, therefore'—such are his very words—' to get rid of their difficulty, have widened the gate of heaven, and allow other ways of arriving there besides that whereby we must be saved. Cato, Socrates, and Aristotle, have been mixed with the number redeemed to God out of every nation,' &c. So speaks Saurin, and so, to be consistent with their principles, all orthodox divines *must* speak.

"Still, as I am willing in the computation before us to be even more than fair, we will allow that one-half the same proportion get to heaven from without Christendom as from within it. Then a sixty-fourth part of Jews, Pagans, and Mahomedans, are conceded to be salvable.

".A sixty-fourth part of eight hundred millions is twelve and a half millions. This
6

is the ratio saved out of these classes every
twenty-five years, and seven hundred and
eighty-seven and a half millions are the
ratio damned. Now sum up the saved and
the lost of a single generation out of the
whole human race. Heaven receives of
them eighteen millions and three fourths—
into the capacious maw of hell nine hundred and eighty-one millions and a fourth
are engulphed! But this is scarcely a unit,
as compared to the grand total of hell's
population.

"Your world, Mr. Tub, taking the Mosaic history to be true, and following the
popular chronology, has subsisted for near
six thousand years; which, divided by
twenty-five—the estimated period of a generation—gives two hundred and forty, as
the number of the generations of man since
time began; and, allowing the relative ratios
of the saved and the lost to have been from
the first what they now are, then, since
time began, the portals of hell have opened
to two hundred and forty times nine hundred and eighty-one and a fourth millions

of doomed spirits! Now you begin to get it, Mr. Tub, but the end is not yet."

"Mr. Paddle, you astound me!" exclaimed Mr. Tub, in astonishment.

"Pardon me," replied the goblin, "you have not heard the twentieth part yet. For first, I have been far more liberal on the side of salvation than facts will warrant. I have, for instance, allowed the same proportion to have gone to heaven before the introduction of Christianity as since, whereas the whole antediluvian world was swept to hell *en masse*, with exceptions scarcely worth considering.

"The gates of perdition swung open to their utmost width on that occasion, Mr. Tub, and whilst those several hundred millions of spirits were pouring in like a continuous flood, the lofty brow of Beelzebub flushed with the proud consciousness of triumph, in having to so large an extent circumvented the plans and purposes of Omnipotence in respect to those numerous offspring of his creative love.

"Moreover, with one fell sweep the communities of Sodom and Gomorrah were transferred to hell; so also were the populations of Babylon, Idumea, Nineveh, Tyre, Sidon, Capernaum, the first-born of Egypt which perished by the last plague, the host that was engulphed in the Red Sea, the hundreds of thousands who were slain by the Israelites in Canaan, the hundred and eighty thousand of Sennacherib's army, slain in one night by the angel of the Lord, the million and more of Jews slain during the siege of Jerusalem, and so on, and so on.

"In full ten thousand instances in the progress of time, have numerous masses of souls been thus consigned to the realms of the damned, but the world of bliss, meanwhile, has received no such accessions.

"Then, again, there were more than twelve centuries that intervened between the Moslem conquests of the territories in Asia and the south of Europe once overspread with Christianity, and the great Reformation under Luther and his co-workers: these are called the 'dark ages,' and during their continuance, so almost total was the depravation of Christendom, that the entire generations of that period, with the exception of here and there an individual, found their way at death to our ungodly abode.

"I tell you in all seriousness, Mr. Tub, that so numerous have been the immigrations to hell from your earth in all past time, that the Devil has felt encouraged to believe that his triumphs in this way would render useless the schemes of Heaven for human redemption, and cause the expiatory sufferings of God's Son to prove a fruitless expenditure"———

"You overwhelmn me, Mr. Paddle!!" again interrupted the elder.

"Patience, my good Triptolemus," resumed the goblin, "your conceptions are not yet expanded to the hundred millionth part of hell's capacity. We have confined our attention, hitherto, to the accessions to hell's population from earth alone; but remember, there was a numerous lapse of spirits from *heaven* itself before your time began. Well, subsequent to that—in the four-thousandth year of time—there was another war in heaven, which resulted in the casting out of a third part of the angels remaining from the former rebellion. In your sacred book (Revelation twelfth) you may find an account of this. Now, allowing an equal portion of the celestial host to have been ejected from heaven at the time of the first revolt, that realm must now contain but one-third of its original inhabitants, and, such being the case in regard to *that* world of reputed perfection, where, as the Omnipotent has his especial abode and his glory is visibly present, one would suppose that the fullest security might be enjoyed—how many myriads of myriads think you—what hosts upon hosts of immortal intelligences —must have fallen at different periods from the innumerable spheres which revolve in the infinitude of space?"——

"Hold! Mr. Paddle, hold!" exclaimed the utterly bewildered, Mr. Tub, "I sink beneath the conception : the sun itself, which in all probability is an inhabited sphere, is a million times larger than our earth, and all the stars are held to be suns of at least equal magnitude, and the centres to separate planetary systems. One hundred millions of these are enumerable by telescopic aid, and who shall affirm that these constitute a millionth part of the universe as visible to the eye of God? I must confess, too, that it seems probable that these are all peopled by beings capable of sinning, and if of sinning, then, also, of incurring a sentence to endless pains. Gracious God! what then *must* be the capacity of that world of despair, if *it* is the sole receptacle for all the outcast spirits of the universe?"

"What must it be, indeed?" resumed Paddle; "it gives me pleasure, my friend, to find that your conceptions are enlarging correspondently to the magnitude of the subject. Why, the magnitude of hell is such that Archimedes, the Syracusian mathematician, has been engaged in an active survey of it ever since his arrival thither, and I heard him say that more than twenty additional centuries must elapse ere his undertaking shall be completed; for, unlike the earth, and other planetary bodies, hell is not measurable by astronomical observations. The almighty architect of the world of suffering knew full well, from the first, for how many myriads of his offspring he was preparing that abode, and he extended its domain accordingly.

"Homer has described Thebes as having a hundred gates; hell has more than a hundred thousand. You will readily believe this, Mr. Tub, when you have duly reflected upon it. Consider, in the first place, the astonishing rapidity of the arrivals thither from this world alone. It is computed that human beings die at the rate of one to every second of time. Sixty, therefore, die every minute; three thousand six hundred every hour; eighty-six thousand four hundred every twenty-four hours! Of these we have already computed the proportion that hell receives.

"It is a subject for solemn thought, Mr. Tub, that every time your heart throbs, at every beat of your pulse—an immortal spirit passes to its final doom! This, from earth alone, mind you. Conceive, now, with what velocity, the gates of woe must swing upon their hinges to admit spirits at this rapid rate! If hell had but a single portal, the arrivals thither from earth alone would keep it opening and shutting with nearly the speed of light. Bethink you, then, how numerous the inlets to hell must necessarily be, to afford ingress to the myriads on myriads, beyond even angelic computation, who are constantly thronging into it from the countless worlds which revolve in immeasurable space!

"But, furthermore, Mr. Tub, you have oft, no doubt, heard your divines argue that God cannot consistently create rational beings without making them morally accountable. If this be so, it holds, of course, in regard to other worlds as well as to this. Accountability implies a liability to sin, and to fall under condemnation. Now it is a doctrine of the church that angels sinned and fell; if such a catastrophe could happen in heaven, the holiest and most blissful seat of existence, why may it not also in all the other worlds throughout the wide immensity? The bard Milton, indeed, has ventured to represent the Deity himself as teaching to the same effect :—

'Sufficient to have stood, though free to fall ;
Such I created all the ethereal powers
And spirits, both them who stood and them who failed.
Freely they stood who stood, and fell who fell.
Not free, what proof could they have given sincer
Of true allegiance, constant faith or love,
Where only what they needs must do appeared,
Not what they would?   What praise could they re-
    ceive ?
What pleasure I from such obedience paid ! '

"It is easy to see, Mr. Tub, that if this
reasoning is good in regard to rational exist-
ences *anywhere*, it is so *everywhere*.   Our
hell is the limbo for convict spirits from
heaven, as well as from earth—why, then,
may it not be such for condemned spirits
from *all* worlds—why not, Mr. Tub?   I
put the case hypothetically, although I am
qualified to state it upon my certain knowledge as a matter of fact; I preferred, however, to satisfy your reason, rather than to
rest a point of such consequence on my
naked declaration.   And if hell is a limbo for
the entire universe, then, my friend, can you
expand your conceptions to the idea of its
magnitude?   Let me assist you.

"The populations of worlds, Mr. Tub,

are, of course, proportionate to their magni-
tudes. I say *of course*, because to suppose
the contrary would be to impeach the wisdom of the almighty architect. If, then,
this globe contains ten hundred millions of
inhabitants, the planet Jupiter, we may
suppose, contains eight hundred times, and
the sun a million times as many. If spirits
pass from those worlds, at the same rapid
rate as from ours, and if a proportion from
them correspondent to that from our world
is damned—and why not?—then, you may
easily calculate, that from Jupiter rushes a
tide of souls into hell at a rate exceeding
four thousand, and from the sun at the rate
of fifty millions per minute!

"Your central luminary, however, vast
as it is, is greatly exceeded in magnitude by
many other suns in the measureless universe, and—but I shall only stupefy and
overwhelm you, sir, with calculations so far
surpassing your limited conceptions. Suffice it, that enough has been said to sustain
my declaration, that this earth, at whose
magnitude you were wondering so much, is

scarcely as big as a hazel-nut in comparison with the vast limbo of the universe"——

"I must here decidedly remonstrate,"
interrupted our elder——

"And, pray, Mr. Tub, what are you a
going to remonstrate about now?" broke in
a third party, in a querulous tone, how
proved none other than our amiable acquaintance, Dorothy. "Do you suppose, Mr.
Tub, that I am to remain alone for hours
in my cold bed, and I suffering with corns
and *rheumatiz?* Let me tell you I 'll do no
such thing—remonstrate or not remonstrate." And Dorothy seated herself in her
arm-chair by the fire, with the air of one
who was bent on indemnifying herself for
the discomfort she had experienced in her
cold and unsocial couch.

By the way—and I mention it for the
benefit of others who may be similarly situated hereafter—it is a pity Dorothy had not
thought of a warming-pan, and a potation
of *yarb* tea; for not only would she have
been likely to realize a comfortable degree

of assistance therefrom, but we, also, would
have been spared the interruption above
recorded, and there is no telling what that
same may have cost us.

Meanwhile the elder wondered what could
have become of Paddle; he at first thought
that he must be confined, in a compressed
state, under the huge bulk of Dorothy, who
may have thrown herself into her chair
without being aware of the presence of its
curious occupant; but he was soon satisfied
that such could not be the case. Paddle
had certainly made his exit from the apartment in some way, whether up the chimney, or, after the manner of fairy queens of
old, through the keyhole, it was impossible
to divine.

The elder, at all events, blessed his stars
that Dorothy had not seen him, inasmuch
as such an event would doubtless have
added hysterics to her chapter of ailments
—to say nothing of the discredit to the
elder's piety from having been found in
company so questionable. So, having ad-
ministered to Dorothy the assistance which
every ailing spouse has a right to expect

7

from her other half, and which she, God bless her, is ever so ready to afford to him, Mr. Tub betook himself to his night's repose.

CHAPTER V.

*In the midst of Elder Tub's ruminations Paddle reappear-
eth, in a fashion beseeming himself and none other—He
anticipateth the remonstrance which was about to be entered
at the close of the last interview, and fully, and satisfactorily, removeth the grounds thereof. Wherefore it
behoveth the reader well to consider this chapter, as he
may herein find his own similar objections to what hath
gone before well and truly answered.*

THE fourth evening from the date at
which this history commences was a cold
and blustering one; Mr. and Mrs. Tub sat
cosily by the fire, enjoying the luxury of
the warmth and cheer within so sensibly
enhanced by contrast with the coldness and
dreariness without. "Paddle will be likely
to stay at home in hell to-night," muttered
the elder, "if thar is half the degree of comfort thar that he reports."

And the elder and Dorothy instinctively
drew nearer the fire, as the wind, which piped
its melancholy notes about the angles, and
through the broad passage of the mansion,

brought ever and anon a pattering of sleet
against the windows, and caused the worthy couple to draw self-comforting compar-
isons between their own condition on that
cold night, and the condition of the poor
whose hearths were fireless, and whose
scanty coverings sufficed not to exclude the
unpitying blasts, which are not gifted with
the moral sense to temper themselves to the
naked and unsheltered. Ah me, the hearts
of the rich, in general, have little advantage to boast over the unpitying blasts in
that respect.

"Yes," mentally ejaculated our hero, as
he sat gazing intently at the red coals in the
grate, and fancifully forming them into various fantastic resemblances; "Paddle will
keep housed in his warm quarters to-night,
but were he to present himself I should not
fail to enforce the remonstrance which Dorothy's untimely appearance prevented me
from urging in our last interview. He is
doubtless right, however, in regard to the
fallibility of all intelligences of all worlds
throughout the universe; for this is the very
idea which parson Smearsoul labored to enforce in his last Sabbath morning sermon.

"'In the case of the angels that kept not their first estate,' said he, 'we have an awful instance that hell is the dread receptacle of spirits from other and higher spheres in the universe, than ours.' He then insisted, by way of vindicating the divine conduct in this matter, that God is under a sort of necessity of creating intelligences morally accountable; and if morally accountable they may sin, and eternally undo themselves. 'To prevent such a catastrophe by force,' said he, 'would be inconsistent with the eternal principles of his nature, and incompatible with the moral freedom and dignity of his creatures.'

"Yes, all that was clar enough to my mind. But as to Paddle's estimate of the proportions saved and damned from this world, I don't believe them; perhaps they hold good as to those who have left the earth in past times; but I have heard the Rev. Mr. Smearsoul make it out clearly, that, in the long run, the saved from earth shall exceed the damned, by as large a difference as thar is between the number of

7*

ference as thar is between the number of convicts in the penitentiaries of a country and the whole residue of its community. This was clarly made out by parson Smear-soul, and tharfore"——

Here the elder stared into the grate—rubbed his eyes—stared again—and again rubbed his eyes. "Can it be," thought he; "*can it, possibly, be?* Why no, that grate wouldn't contain the whole person of Paddle, and yet thar he seems to be, sure enough, perfect in all his form and features." And the elder looked in alarm toward Dorothy, to see if she also was not a witness to the appearance of his strange visitant. But Dorothy's soul was in the realm of Somnus, and little chance there seemed, from the deep trumpet-notes emitted from her nasal organ, that any ordinary occurrence would suffice to disenchant her from the spell of the sleeping god.

Paddle, meanwhile, sat amid the red coals with as stoical an indifference to their heat, as is evinced by an Indian warrior to the devices of torture practised upon him by his captors. His countenance wore its usually comical leer, and his deep-set optics twinkled with their usually humorous expression.

"*He, he!* my friend Triptolemus," exclaimed the goblin, "you are marvellously gullible! All mortals are, for that matter. The devil finds easy work in getting them into his traps; and the wonder is that the Creator, who professedly is so desirous of their eternal good, should have exposed them to the wiles of a foe who is so capable of outwitting them!

"It really, friend Tub, puts my gravity to severe proof to witness the efforts of your theologians at the present day, who, finding that the good old doctrine of endless damnation is losing its savour among men, and bringing the goodness of God into question, put all their ingenuity on the strain in order to prove that, in the long run, the number of the saved of mankind will immensely exceed that of the damned!

"They come at this result by a marvellously curious process of numeration. 'First,' say they, 'all are saved who die in infancy. Then, all the heathen, Jews, Mahomedans, and so forth, who rightly improve their advantages. Then, again, there is by and by to come a millennium —a thousand years' reign of Christ on the earth—during which everybody is to be righteous. Furthermore, this thousand years may mean'—mark, it *may* mean— 'just three hundred and sixty-five thousand years instead of one thousand!' For what reason it may so mean does not clearly appear—except, perchance, that it is very necessary to the hypothesis.

"And so, by this *hocus pocus* process of computation it is made out—quite to the satisfaction of those who wish to have it so —that the number of the finally saved of mankind will immeasurably exceed that of the lost. How stupidly blind must the herd of believers be presumed to be by the priests who manage their spiritual matters!

"Now, Mr. Tub, though a goblin of the lower pit, I am sorry to see your sacred book so poorly interpreted. Suppose, now, we even admit that a millennium is literally to take place—though this, by the great majority of Christians, is denied. Suppose, farther, that we admit its duration will be just three hundred and sixty-five times as long as the literal description warrants—and that, again, is exceedingly questionable. Nevertheless, with so much granted, it still remains to be proved that everybody will be righteous during its continuance.

"Hear the following quotation, Mr. Tub, and judge how difficult would be their task who should attempt such proof. '*And when the thousand years are expired, Satan shall be loosed from his prison, and shall go out to deceive the nations which are in the four quarters of the earth, Gog and Magog, to gather them together to battle, the number of whom is as the sand of the sea. And they went up on the breadth of the earth, and compassed the camp of the saints about, and the beloved city, and fire came down from heaven and devoured them.*'

"Hence you see, Mr. Tub, that at the termination of this boasted era of Messiah's reign on earth, a multitude equalling the sea-sands in number is to be added to the population of hell. When did that of heaven ever receive such an accession? Those wise heads amongst you, therefore, who are so liberal in their calculations on heaven's side, must find some better data therefor than the Bible furnishes, or common sense either.

" But let us take them, now, on their own principles, Mr. Tub, and see, as respects Mahomedans, Jews, and heathen, *to* what result we shall fairly come. The Bible itself tells us that *no man cometh to the Father except by Christ*—his is *the only name given under heaven among men whereby they must be saved;* and the sacred record expressly adds, *neither is there salvation in any other.* Now these divines, Mr. Tub, profess to take this book as their authority.—By the way, my friend, it is more read, and better understood, in hell than on earth. That heathens do not in this life come to God by Christ, is certain. That they are not here born again—or, in other words, born into the kingdom of Christ, is also certain. It is equally so, according to these gentlemen, that *there is no change after death.* Now, according to these principles, let them get the heathen to heaven if they can. *He, he!* Let them see to it that it is not all a trick of the devil to prevent themselves from getting there.

"As to infants, we shall not dispute about their all going to paradise when they die; but I cannot forbear the remark that if God looked to the interests of his kingdom as sharply as the devil does to *his*, he would cause a great many more to die in infancy than now do—*all*, for example, who, living to maturity, he foresees will ultimately be damned. The devil would thus be defrauded of millions of souls which he now contrives to secure to himself.

"The elect in your younger days, Mr. Tub, would have scouted as an impious heresy the notion that more will be saved than damned; it was the essence of their comfort to believe that heaven is a snug little walled city, with jasper gates and streets of gold, where saints and angels shall have nothing to do to all eternity but to sit on great benches and sing psalms.

"And the company of the place, you may remember, was to be a number ' so fixed and definite, as to be incapable of increase or diminution.' Great comfort took the

saints of that day in singing Watts' metri-
cal paraphrase of the text concerning the
broad and narrow roads.

'Broad is the road that leads to death,
And thousands flock together there,
But wisdom shows a narrow path
With here and there a traveller.'

It was one saved to thousands damned in
those good old times, Mr. Tub, but the
orthodoxy of the church is now heels upper-
most.

"It was then believed that not a Jew, nor
a Mahomedan, nor a Pagan, nor an infant,
except of elect parents—nor then except
baptized—nor a Socinian, nor a Methodist,
nor a Papist, would ever be so fortunate as to
get to heaven. But of late, either heaven
has grown more capacious, or the terms of
admission have got to be more easy, or the
gate-keeper has become remiss in examin-
ing the passports; for by a late census of
the place your wise-headed divines have
ascertained that its population outnumbers
that of hell, by as much as that of the honest portion of a community does that of the
convict portion in its penitentiaries!

"*He, he!* At this rate, Mr. Tub, we nall all be in heaven by-and-by, the devil iimself will be saved, and the great bonfire put out, which, at the expense of so much sulphur, has been kept burning so long for the accommodation of wicked and heretical spirits. Only keep on improving your theology, and that will be the upshot of it some day.

"And this reminds me, Mr. Tub, that of late years some queer geniuses have arrived amongst us, who, when on earth, used to explain texts of holy writ which speak of hell, everlasting fire, &c., as pertaining only to severe temporal punishments, and as having no reference to a condition of misery beyond death. They also used to insist that righteousness is eventually to become universal, in all states of existence, and that union, love, and happiness, will prevail throughout the universe. These queer personages were for taking everybody to heaven eventually, and really, Mr. Tub, their theory, though, of course, heretical, is pleasing, plausible, and hangs remarkably well together.

8

" *He, he!* they are all of them damned
for the heresy as fast as they leave the
world, and little good will does the devil
owe them for predicting his own final overthrow, and for having denied his very existence among men. Nevertheless, they come
to our place with good, loving dispositions,
which their heresy is well adapted to inspire,
and they make, on the whole, a very correct and orderly class of citizens; for they
still adhere to the notion that well-*doing*
secures well-*being;* nor can they, even in
hell, be divested of the notion that God is
too good to permit any evil, out of which
good shall not ultimately arise; and consequently, they persist in expecting a happy
termination to the sufferings in hell, both of
themselves and all others. Now that, Mr.
Tub, I call a good, liberal, and neighborly
sort of faith ; when *they* are saved, *all* will
be. That should put to shame your narrow, Calvinistic ejaculations—' Lord, make
me one of those *heres and theres!*' However, the devil don't like it, and is at as
much pains to prevent its spreading in hell,

as the priests are to obstruct its diffusion on earth."

I take it not on me to say how long Paddle would have kept his tongue running if no interruption had occurred, for there seemed no end to his subject-matter; but Dorothy's organs pealed forth so stentorian a note at this stage of the interview that it aroused her out of her sleep, and her *rhumatiz* at the same time giving her an extra twitch, it was clear enough to the elder that no further communications could take place for that evening in which his amiable help-meet should not be a party.

The elder naturally turned an anxious glance at the grate, to see if it still contained his singular visitant. There he still seemed to be! There was his outline—his countenance—his grinning features—his leering eyes! Did Dorothy see him? She, too, was looking straight into the fire; yet her entire composure made it evident that the goblin was not visible to her!

How was it? Did Mr. Tub's eyes deceive him? To test that point he took up the poker, and—carefully at first, lest he might seem to Paddie to be making a personal attack on him- he began to stir the coals. To his great astonishment nothing was there, but a fanciful outline which the elder's imagination had been all along regarding as the actual presence of his goblin acquaintance! "It's clar enough to me now," mentally exclaimed the puzzled elder, "that I am bewitched—thar can be no mistake about it."

So thinks the author of this history, also —nay, he is sure of it, and equally so that the reader hereof will be of the same persuasion. It is an easy thing for one to form in a fire of coals—in a certain condition—whatever fantastic forms one pleases; and having fancied a human figure to be there, it is easy to conceive it as speaking, and to frame language for it, answerable to the ideas we may conceive of its character.

All this, the reader knows, is easy; I say not that such were really the facts in the elder's case; I merely furnish the philosophical key, and with it the reader may unlock the mystery as liketh him best.

CHAPTER VI.

*Wherein the philosophic Paddle doth marvellously enlighten
our elder in regard to the devil and other sacred subjects.
He also taketh unseemly liberties with what divers godly
persons have set forth on the same heads, whereupon it
would appear—if the thing were credible—that even godly
men may sometimes be mistaken. Moreover, Paddle ex-
poundeth certain opinions which are current in the infernal world, and reasoneth thereupon in a way which will no
fail to edify the unprejudiced reader.*

OVER against the elder's farm there is a
range of hills on the Ohio side, between
which and the river-bank runs a narrow
and irregular strip of lower ground—not
entirely level—which is in part of alluvial
formation, and in part formed of the soil that
the rains have washed down those steep de-
clivities. On that narrow esplanade our elder
arrived on the fifth evening of our narrative,
just as the twilight was deepening into
darkness, and the forms and colors of objects were becoming dim and indistinct.

8*

" Halloo——the skiff!" bawled the elder
" Be sharp there, Cesar, and hurry over."

" De skiff no yere, marsa," hallood Cesar
in return. "Missus went over to de island
wiv it, to take tea wiv missus Strawbottom,
and she no comed home yet—'spec Sambo
yere wiv her ebery minute."

" D——" The elder was on the point of
swearing, but he did not; it is with great
pleasure that I record the fact of his for-
bearance. Truth is—and I state it here as
an illustration of the vast utility of being
born again—as the elder was on the point
of venting a bad word, it occurred to him
that, being a Christian elder, it would be
decidedly unbecoming; and, besides, how
near at hand the devil might be to overhear
him, he knew not—for, for *some* reason, we
are apt to be more apprehensive on that
score in the darkness than in the light. So
our elder suffered his impatience to expend
itself in *thinking* the word to which he had
piously refrained from giving expression.

" *He, he!* " tittered Shadrach Paddle,
who just then became visible seated at his
ease on the sward with his back against

a stump. "It is a great virtue to take things coolly, elder Tub; I used to teach the same doctrine when alive, to my good friend Epaphroditus, your father, who was of a choleric turn, as you also seem to be. Persons of that temper, Mr. Tub, don't usually make very good saints—they need to be too often converted over again, and that, you know, involves quite a waste of grace.

> ' Now I repent and sin again ;
> Now I revive, and now I 'm slain.'

So sings one of them, and he was but a type of a large tribe of saints"——

"Mr. Paddle," interrupted the elder, in a tone of some alarm. "I fear your several visits to me are for no good; the thoughts you have already put into my head would materially injure my standing in the church if I should give utterance to them. There is scarcely anything of which I could be guilty, indeed—not even swearing, lying, or cheating a customer—that will so jeopardize my church standing as the sin of heresy. I have just returned from a visit to deacon Splawfoot, who is a very particular friend of mine, as I supply my stock of liquors from his distillery. I told him in confidence of your several visits to me, and he gave it as his decided opinion that you are the devil. 'For the devil,' said he, 'can assume any form that best suits his purpose, from that of a snake (as in Eden) to that of an angel of light,' "——

"Pooh, pooh !" broke in the goblin, rising from the sward and seating himself on the stump against which he had been propping his back, while the elder, at his motion, seated himself on another near at hand. "It's little your deacon Strawbottom knows about these things, Mr. Tub, for the devil has no need to be in the premises where a still-house is doing his work without him. You are compelled to await the arrival of the skiff, Mr. Tub, and, you cannot more profitably employ the interval than in listening to your father's old chum, Shadrach Paddle.

"*He, he!*" tittered the goblin in continuation, after indulging for a few moments in silent mirthfulness. "It is a prodigious pity, Mr. Tub, that your wise divines have

not settled it in ecclesiastical council whether the devil be black, white, or gray;
whether he is ox-hoofed, or ass-hoofed; confined, or at large; and many other particu-
lars about which opinion is strangely contra-
dictory. ｡Some awkward incongruities arise
among mortals from the lack of accurate
information on these points.

"Your English devil, for instance, is
cloven-footed, and however well he may
disguise the other parts of his person, he
cannot, it seems, conceal the parted hoof.
Now the Dutch, on the contrary, ascribe to
their devil a hoof like a horse. According
to the former representation, he is an eata-
ble animal by the provisions of the Mosaic
statutes—allowing he also chews the cud;
whereas according to the latter he is included
amongst unclean beasts. *He, he!* Your
parsons must see to it, Mr. Tub, that their
people are kept right in regard to the devil;
he will otherwise fade from human faith as
ghosts, witches, fairies, ogres, and the like
already have in a large portion of Christendom.

".Even now, Mr. Tub, your saints are

'ess wise in regard to the devil than they
used to be half a century ago; neither are
they as much dogged through life by him as
were the saints of former times. ·Poor souls,
they had little peace of their lives for the
devil; and—*he, he!*—in spite of all the aid
they could get from God and his Spirit, and
their fellow saints, he oft tripped up their
feet, and gave them such a souse into the
slough of iniquity that it cost a large expenditure of heavenly grace to restore them to
a decent degree of cleanliness. However,
they took large comfort in thinking that the
more numerous their conflicts with the
devil the greater was their sanctity; hence,
in their autobiographies you find marvellous
records of their feats in that way.

"They all the while held, nevertheless—
and that illustrates how well the different
parts of a pure, evangelic faith hang together—that Satan is closely confined in hell,
and unable, by his utmost exertions, to ex-
tricate himself from his fiery prison. Hence
they say in one of their hymns:

' There Satan, the first sinner, lies,
    And roars, and bites his iron bands,
In vain the rebel strives to rise,
    Crushed with the weight of both thy hands.'

As if the´ Almighty—*he, he !*—unable to hold the devil down in the fire with one hand, must needs employ two for the purpose!

"Truth is though, Mr. Tub, the devil is entitled to heavy damages for defamation from that tribe of gentlemen, for they assail his character with unscrupulous license; Clarke, the commentator, for instance, asserts that it was probably he who raised the tempest about the vessel in which Messiah and his disciples were sailing, with the purpose of sinking the whole concern together, and thus quashing the gospel scheme in its beginning! A most shrewd design no doubt; but it supposes the devil a greater fool than he has been taken for, to hope any advantage to his cause from a tempest which he knew Messiah had ample power to calm! For a knave the devil is known all the world over; but nobody mistrusts him for a fool.

"*He, he!* not by any means. For consider, Mr. Tub, how shrewdly he contrived
to get our first mother to eat the interdicted
apple—

——————— ' whose mortal taste
Brought death into the world, with all our woes ;'

as the bard Milton has it. *He, he!* apples
must have been scarce in those days, and
souls very cheap; since one of the former
cost the endless damnation of so many myriads of the latter.   And what goes farther
to illustrate Satan's tact in the affair is, that
according to the poet aforenamed, it was to
supply the gap in heaven's population occasioned by the rebellion and banishment of
the rebel angels, that the race of man was
created !   And yet Satan has contrived to
profit a million times more largely by it
than has the Creator himself !"——

"Forbear, Mr. Paddle ! forbear !" interpos-
ed the elder, rising from his seat on the stump
with the energy of his indignant astonishment. "The most sacred and solemn truths
of our religion cease to appear such, so soon
as they are touched by the scathing bolts of
your sarcasm. My belief in these awful

mysteries, Mr. Paddle, is feeble at best; and if I listen to you longer I shall be a heretic outright, which would be much against my interests, seeing that it would lose me the countenance and custom of all the evangelical Christians in the neighborhood, and they are a large majority"——

"Be composed, my good Mr. Tub, and fear nothing from your father's old friend," answered the goblin; "and as to heresy upon these points, why, keep it to yourself as others do—such is now the fashion of the times. The faith of this day has a less capacious gullet in the strictest believers than had the faith of former times; the latter swallowed whatever was given to it under the stamp of orthodoxy, however huge; it would not have choked in the effort to believe that Jonah swallowed a whale. Not it; for had the impossibility of the thing been demonstrated, its certain recourse would have been to spiritualize the whale, and take the story down in that shape.

"Even your parson Smearsoul's faith, Mr. Tub, is troubled with the difficulty of swallow which is now so generally prevalent. He was reading Benson's Commentary a few days since on the text, "If I make my bed in hell, thence also shall thy hand lead me, and thy right hand shall guide me.' The commentator maintains from hence that God is present in hell for a two-fold purpose. First, to blow up its fires to their utmost intensity; and secondly, to quicken the sensibilities of the damned, in order that they may be keenly alive to the tortures of that fiery lake!

"Satan was at the parson's elbow at that moment, and he whispered him, 'There's for you, parson Smearsoul; there's a picture of the Deity by one of his own saints. Would you know it from a picture of the devil?'

"The good man started up—lodged his pen on his ear—strided to and fro across his study—and wrestled desperately with heretical surmises for a few minutes. 'However,' concluded he at length, 'my province is to *preach* these doctrines, true or false; it is by that craft I have my living; orthodoxy, I find to comport vastly with my personal comfort; whereas to be a heretic would lose

me the affection and fleece of my flock so
soon as it should be discovered.'

"And so he resumed his seat with a res-
olute determination to believe everything
contained in his evangelical authorities, be
it what it would. There's a lesson in the
science of credulity for you, Mr. Tub; follow it, and you are sure to be on the major
side in faith on all subjects.

"Well, heresy is on the increase, Mr.
Tub, even in hell; we have of late, numerous arrivals of the class of Christians afore
described, whose error consisted in sup-
posing that God is good enough to take care
of all the souls he has made. The rogues
have the audacity to back up their notion
with a strong force of Scripture testimony.
Even after their arrival among us they still
persist in their heresy—for there is, you
know, *no change after death*—and they
insist that hell will be destroyed in due
time; all heresies cease; sin, suffering, the
devil, and all other bad things be brought
to an end; and all souls be brought to
a happy and harmonious house-keeping
together, with God, and his Son, and angels,
in heaven forever and ever.

" The thing sounds very well, Mr. Tub—
does it not? Why they should be sent to
hell for entertaining such pleasant opinions
seems strange; but, it seems, from all that
priests tell us, that the Deity has a dreadful
spite against those who mistake their creed.
And this accounts why holy men on earth
have made so many bonfires for the accommodation of the same class—it was but
affording them a foretaste of the comforts
of the great bonfire below—and who shall
deny to the saints the prerogative of imi-
tating their God? They have been born
again, you know, and like father like children.

" Now, we have in hell some very ancient
religionists, known on earth as Manicheans,
whose creed strikingly resembled what is
now a pure evangelical faith, so far, at
least, as respects the origin and endless continuance of good and evil. This sect once
flourished extensively over the south-west-
ern portion of Asia. Their personified Principle of Evil, the origin of darkness, misery,
death, and so on, corresponds closely to
the devil of the popular Christian creed.

And their Good Principle—the originator of light, and purity, and all approvable things, was as powerless against his antagonist, as is Jehovah against the devil. Consequently, they held as evangelic Christians do—that evil shall be as eternal in its duration as good.

"But, then, on the part of the Manicheans there was more consistency in so holding, for, as these opposing principles were equal, it was not to be expected that the one should ever be able to overcome the other; whereas, on the part of evangelic Christians, Jehovah is held to be infinite and the devil to be finite. Yet the latter, and his works, shall eternally coendure with the former, and the unoriginated principles of his moral nature! *He, he!* the faith that swallows these beautiful consistencies without choking, deserves, sure enough, to be rewarded with the privilege of singing psalms to all eternity.

"Well, we have grand debates on these several subjects in hell, Mr. Tub. Of our powers in that way you have a sample in the 'Paradise Lost,' of Milton; who farther

9*

informs you that after the breaking up of the great council, in which they debated the question of peace or war with the Deity; some of the rebel angels betook themselves to one employment, and some to another.

> ' Others, apart, sat on a hill retired,
>   In thoughts more elevate, and reasoned high
>   Of providence, foreknowledge, will, and fate.'

And we have plenty of the masters of logic there, Mr. Tub; Aristotle, with his sylogisms; the author of the Socratian method also, as well as our American sage who was such an adept therein. Then we have the Academicians, the Sophists, the"————·

"Marsa—de skiff coming!" rang out at this moment on the silent evening air, and bounded in echoes from hill to hill. The elder sprang up gladly at the sound, and as he did so he found that the neighboring stump also had been suddenly deserted by its occupant. To that which he had occupied he found, by feeling, that some warmth had been communicated by his body; but on that which had supported the goblin the evening dew lay moist and cold.

" Paddle cannot possibly have been seated thar all this time," muttered the 'elder; "the night-dew could not have fallen thar through his person at this rate—the thing is clarly impossible, and——Well Cesar, you are here—are you? Very well; hurry over. now, for I am chilled and want my supper."

So ended the affair of the fifth evening; the reader is left to form his own free opinion about it; and he is quite as capable of doing so, it is hoped, as is his humble servant, the narrator.

CHAPTER VII.

Paddle's last visit, wherein he assumeth, with a sort of Dutch-uncle freedom, to be wiser in regard to the means and chances of salvation, than are even pious ministers whose trade it is to be so. He also indulgeth an impious license of remark on many mysterious matters connected with the popular form of Christianity, for the which he will not be likely to obtain credit with the godly reader Nevertheless, it was deemed fitting that the same should be recorded, since it illustrateth the sophistries with which Satan is wont to assail pious ears, in order to the shaking of their faith in the mysteries of their holy religion. The elder confesseth a leaning to heresy, in the private ears of his spouse Dorothy, and this leadeth to a satisfactory clearing up of the matter of Paddle's appearances.

"AHEM! Out late this evening, Mr. Tub —hope you've profited by the wholesome communications of your friend Paddle, for you are to be favored with no more of them after to-night. You must therefore 'give the more earnest heed to the things you have heard, lest at any time you should let them slip;' these things, Mr. Tub, will make you 'wise unto'—but no matter what

—I marvellously incline to be scriptural to-night—a natural result of my serious habits, no doubt."

Thus was our elder addressed on his way from church one misty evening, whither he had been for several successive preceding days and nights to hear the Rev. Asaph Spume, who had worked up quite a revival in Parson Smearsoul's church. Now this the Rev. Asaph aforesaid could do in any church whatever, for he had the remarkable faculty of taking the Holy Ghost with him to wheresoever he had contracted to get up a revival. Parson Smearsoul had not such faculty; he had therefore engaged his reverend brother Spume to do the thing for him —which was very proper, of course.

On the evening aforesaid a chilly mist was falling, through which the moonbeams struggled with a faint and sickly light, which barely enabled our hero to perceive that the incorrigible Paddle was at his side, and mounted on a horse which, whether he quickened his gait or retarded it, kept exactly even pace with his own.

" Mr. Paddle," said the elder, " I would

not like the comfortable frame of my mind
disturbed at present by the matters to which
you allude : I have been listening to a most
edifying discourse about the devil, and his,
various devices for entrapping newly converted souls, of which several have been
added to the church during this gracious
outpouring.   That precious man, the Rev.
Asaph Spume, is remarkably acquainted
with the numerous tricks and stratagems of
Satan"——

"And reason good," interrupted Paddle;
"the godly man has much connexion with
him, and is often caught in his net.   And
suppose you, Mr. Tub, that the devil was
not present whilst he was thus preached
about?   Let me tell you, the sermon had no
auditor more wakefully attentive thereto
than was he; and the chances are many
that he whispered in the preacher's ear at
the close, 'What a splendid sermon!
Everybody must have admired it. See how
the eyes of those fair sisters are sparkling
on you with admiration!   Such talents
must win you favor everywhere, and bring
you so much into requisition that you may

assure yourself of plenty of honor and emolument.'

"For the devil being a free commoner all over creation, Mr. Tub, is always at hand where, and when, he conceives his services to be most necessary. That he is an old and regular church-goer you may learn from the sacred oracles; for as long ago as in Job's day, 'when the sons of God came up to present themselves before the Lord, Satan came also amongst them.' Hence, a quaint old couplet saith most truly, that—

> 'There's nowhere found a house of prayer,
> But Satan hath an altar there.'

Your old divines were all well aware of this : hence, when Whitefield was once informed that he had preached a very able sermon, he replied that the devil had so informed him before he came out of the pulpit. So you see, Mr. Tub, that the devil was very probably present while brother Spume was so dexterously exposing his arts to your people."

Paddle paused, and the two continued to jog along side by side in silence for half a mile or so, when the elder, remembering the direction of Mr. Spume, that when the devil comes with his evil suggestions it is best to ejaculate short prayers, or to sing a verse or two of some solemn hymn, broke forth into the following fragmentary stanzas :—

" Dangers stand thick thro' all the ground
    To push us to the tomb,
And fierce diseases wait around
    To hurry mortals home.

Great God, on what a slender thread
    Hang everlasting things !
Th' eternal states of all the dead
    Upon life's feeble strings.

Infinite joy, or endless woe,
    Depends on every breath,
And yet"———

" Hold up awhile, Mr. Tub," broke in the goblin, "and allow me to ask, *who* hung those everlasting things on that slender thread ? The Creator himself, of course, and of course, too, he knew how slender the thread was, and how momentous were the interests dependent on it ! Surely, then, he must have held those interests very cheaply to nave suspended them upon a contingence so brittle! *He, he!* Mr. Tub, this is another of those views of God afforded by your evangelical creeds, which make Satan himself to look amiable in the comparison.

"*He, he!* infinite things dependent on a breath! I should like to know, my good friend Tub, what thoughts Shadrach Paddle could put into your head that could make you think worse of God than that comes to. Nevertheless, so teaches your creed, Mr. Tub, and the creed is true of course; it is the creed we most like in hell· it pictures forth God agreeably to our notions, and—as before hinted—the devil has no sort of liking for the heretics who hold that he and his realm are to be finally abolished—all evil made subservient to eventual good, and the whole universe to become holy and happy. No, Mr. Tub, this heresy finds no favor with Satan at all; and he would no doubt deal rigorously with those of his subjects who hold to it, were it not that God's saints have practised persecution on earth to such an extent that the devil has become disgusted at it.

10

'Infinite joy or endless woe,
Depends on every breath.'

So they do, Mr. Tub, sure enough: how many, for instance, now in heaven, owe their being there to the lucky accident of their having died in infancy; and how many in hell would have been in the other country, too, if they had been equally fortunate. The merest accident in the world decides the momentous alternative—

' A point of time—a moment's space,
Removes us to that heavenly place,
Or shuts us up in hell.'

Your humble servant, Shadrach Paddle, thinks, that if *he* had been at the trouble of making immortal beings, he would have taken better care of them than to stake their weal or woe forever upon such slender chances; more especially if, in addition to creating, he had been also at the trouble and expense of redeeming them.

"And, then, moreover, don't you think it is bad economy in mortals, also, Mr. Tub, to be at such large pains and cost to rear their children to man and womanhood, at

the risk of their going to the devil at last,
when, should they die in infancy, they are
sure of going straight to heavenly bliss?
He, he! The devil profits hugely by the
indifference of the Creator in this matter on
the one hand, and the folly of parents on
the other"——

"Mr. Paddle, I can't allow that," interrupted elder Tub. " Your ridicule, I
acknowledge, applies mighty well against
Arminians; because, according to them, God
has left everything at loose ends—all is.
mighty uncertain in thar system, I confess.
But I believe, Mr. Paddle, in a 'covenant
ordered in all things and sure;' the children
of the elect are sanctified in thar believing
parents; thar's no Arminian chance about
it, Mr. Paddle; 'God, from all eternity, fore-
ordains' "——

"Pooh, pooh! elder Tub;" broke in the
goblin, "I am not agoing to bandy argu-
ments with you on election and reprobation;
I speak what I know when I assert, that
the merest chance imaginable makes the
scale, in each individual's case, to prepon-
derate for endless glory or endless flames.

Why, I could cite you facts without number to this point. Take one as a 'sample; to which your father was personally knowing, as well as myself, for it occurred in the part of Old Virginia whence we both came.

" Toby Tibbins was convicted of being a tory spy, and sentenced to be hung as such. Well, Toby turned to and got religion, for he thought it would be a hard case to be damned as well as hung. He therefore, with the help of the several parsons thereabout, got his spiritual affairs in good and safe trim. The fellow had a melodious voice, and when I visited him in prison I thought it doubtful if Gabriel himself could beat him far in psalm-singing. Unluckily for his soul, however—though a comfortable thing enough for his neck—he was pardoned under the gallows, in consideration of some useful service he had rendered to our army in a particular case. Toby, who has been long in hell with us, has often told your father and me that, but for that pardon, the devil would certainly have been one soul out of pocket; for he had got safely through being born again, and had obtained his ticket for heaven.

"Take another: Obadiah Snubs had a natural turn for religion; he was soundly converted several different times; but his misfortune was that his nose was set too far on one side of his face, and that same nose was a serious hindrance to his soul's salvation, for it involved him in constant broils. Well, Obadiah moved at length to this western district, (then a wilderness,) where he hoped to escape the ridicule to which his nasal organ had subjected him east of the mountains. So he squatted in a cabin near Grave Creek; in which retirement he managed to keep his soul's affairs in a safe condition for some time; but, having occasion to go to Fort Wheeling one day to buy stores, a fellow there took the liberty to make invidious remarks on the awry posture of his unfortunate proboscis; which so enraged poor Obadiah, that—forgetting that he was converted, and all that—he drew his knife on his tormentor, and was killed in the quarrel. Now, Mr. Tub, would not Oba-

10*

diah Snubs have been now in heaven but for that luckless nose ?

"You have been having a protracted meeting in your church.—The devil, mind you, was a regular attendant thereat.—You witnessed the ghostly gloom with which holy men clothe their countenances for the occasion—you have seen how, with upturned eyes, and sepulchral whispers, and pantomimic gestures, they have labored to strike awe into weak minds, and produce the impression that God is there and at work. You might also hear the timid heart beating with vibrations of terror, in the bosoms of the more credulous and susceptible among the auditors; and as with stealthy step the aisles are paced to and fro by the crafty agents in the business, one terror-stricken female after another is induced to go up and occupy the 'anxious benches.'

"Now—mark you, my friend—the whole work is God's—the Almighty God's—and the salvation of immortal souls is its sole end. But—*he, he!*—can you doubt that the least ludicrous incident—such as a pig squeaking in at one of the windows, or a monkey grinning over the breastwork of the pulpit—would convert the whole business into a broad farce, and defeat heaven of a score or two of souls? *He, he!* Well, indeed, might the afore-quoted balladist exclaim—

————— 'On what a slender thread
Hang everlasting things.'

I must repeat, elder Tub, that if I had been at the trouble of creating such things, I should have hung them over hell less slenderly, except I held them in so cheap an estimation that it would little concern me whether they were saved or damned.

"Yes, elder Tub, say what you will, the merest accident determines the fate of the soul forever. Why, even I—Shadrach Paddle—graceless as I may now seem, came very near being born again at one time; I should have made it out, I believe, but that the devil, finding that I had a strong natural turn for whatever was comical, took care to put funny thoughts into my head when I was saying my prayers; and that, of course, spoiled the whole proceeding.

"Among our lecturers in hell, we have,

recently, some odd geniuses, whose custom
it is to visit graves and take casts of skulls.
On these they theorize as to the characters,
mental and moral, of the individuals to
whom, in life, they belonged; and it is amaz-
ing with what nice discrimination they
analyze and define the mental and moral
powers, and exhibit the influence exerted
upon each individual's destiny by his peculiar cranial conformation.

" For example, an acquaintance of mine
on earth, now in hell, was remarkably pious
for the first forty years of his life; my intimacy with him fully convinced me that his
piety was sincere.   Nevertheless, and much
to my surprise, he came to hell at death, having lived a sinner for a year and a half previous thereto.   The devil got great credit in
hell for his supposed adroitness in thus up-
setting, in relation to that individual, the
whole work of the Holy Spirit for forty
years.   It happened, however, that one of
the geniuses afore-mentioned visited the
fellow's grave, and took a cast of his skull,
from whence he made it clearly to appear,
that the sudden loss of his religion had been

occasioned by the accident of a blow on the head from a falling brick, which had completely depressed his organ of veneration. Thus was the mystery explained; for the religious sentiment is known to be feeble where that organ is deficient.

"Nor are you even sure of remaining in heaven, Mr. Tub, after you have safely run all the hazards of getting there. If, as the hymn has it—

'From heaven the sinning angels fell,'

what hinders that sinning saints may be tumbling from there, too? You are free agents here, and, you know, *there is no change after death.* Now such a fall would not be much to your comfort, Mr. Tub; if Milton be correct, it requires

'Nine times the space that measures day and night
  To mortal man,'

to get over the distance between the two countries, and that is an inconveniently long time to be tumbling, to say nothing of the uncomfortable change of climate experienced at the end of it"——

"But the Rev. Mr. Smearsoul says," put in the elder, "that thar's no more possibility of sinning, after we have served out our probation"——

"I care not," retorted Paddle, "what your parson Smearsoul says; he knows nothing about it. Then, as infants serve *no* probation here, they must serve it hereafter, probably. Moreover, as some die pious at an early age, and go to heaven, while others serve God for scores of years, before they die; either the former must serve their probation faster, or, dying ere it is closed, finish it in heaven; or the latter must close it before they die, and what they do after is over-work!

"Truth is, Mr. Tub, your theology is all in a snarl—it is an inextricably tangled affair. *He, he!* It seems, then, that they who have safely run the gantlet through the traps and wiles of the devil in this world, are, in another, treated like the old pensioners upon government, whose wounds and length of service secure them a support at the public expense, and an exemption from military enrolment in future to the end of their days.

'Well-a-day! There are many curiosities connected with these matters; and therefore is it that human reason is forbidden to poke her impertinent nose too far into them. For instance, there is coming a future general judgment, at which saints and sinners—whom death had severed, and kept apart by an impassable gulf long before—are to be separated from each other; and their causes, which had long before been decided by the infallible Judge, shall then undergo a readjudication! We are committed for the present only on suspicion it seems: it may turn out that some of us have been suffering false imprisonment during the intermediate term. *He, he!* if such shall chance to appear in the cases of Shadrach Paddle and his wife Dolly, what a comfortable thing it will be! For, to say truth, Mr. Tub, although hell is a very tolerable place, taking it all in all; yet I think there are climates that would better agree with mine and Dolly's constitutions. I find, indeed, that climate has a great deal to do with the agreeableness of a country; and nell, I must confess, is not remarkably blest in that respect. Dolly and I, therefore, are

made up to emigrate, if the mistake alluded
to shall appear to have been made in our
cases.

"You are one of the elect, Mr. Tub, and,
at the great day of judgment aforenamed,
when sentence of endless damnation shall
be pronounced against Epaphroditus Tub,
your father, and Tabitha Tub, your mother, it will be your duty—so sermon-books
say—to pronounce thereupon a loud and
emphatic AMEN! If you don't feel like doing this, you have reason to suspect the
genuineness of your conversion. Nay, more
than that, you must even be willing to be
damned yourself, provided that the matter
of eternally roasting Triptolemus Tub is
seen to be necessary to the glory of God.

"Well, here we are, at your gate, Mr.
Tub, and there stands your negro awaiting
his master, poor fellow, while this chilly
mist has gradually soaked his scanty cover-
ing to the.skin. But no matter; negroes
were only made for white people's conven-
ience. I have a few parting maxims for
you, Mr. Tub, and shall then take my
leave.

"Don't put off repentance too long, after some special act of knavery, lest you might die meanwhile and your soul be cheated of heaven. Have as little to do with conscience as possible—a man who keeps a store and tavern can rarely afford to harbor so troublesome an article—and, for the matter of that, it is a bore at best. The devil's turnpike abounds with posies, preachers say; therefore, keep as near thereto as is at all consistent with walking the narrow road, and pluck as many as you can without too much endangering your soul. Belief of the truth is well enough, provided you can find a large majority to believe it with you; but, as to believing with the minority, seldom is anything gained thereby, save a brand in this life, and damnation in the life to come. Let the thermometer of your piety vary with the religious temperature of the times; for then will it be always at the proper and profitable degree, whether up at fever heat or down at zero. A scrupulous faith is seldom profitable; but a faith which gorges whole systems, without regard to particu-

11

lars, is the faith which the clergy most affect
and patronize.

"I could largely multiply these maxims,
Mr. Tub, did time permit; by practising
upon them you run, 'tis true, some risk
of going to the devil at last; but they are
found, it is said, vastly convenient for this
life; and I should judge as much myself,
from the fact that they are, and always
have been, so much in fashion. But you,
my good Triptolemus, are already apt in
these matters, as are also the most of your
fellow-saints. So, good-bye to you, Mr.
Tub."

"Did you see him, Cesar?" inquired the
elder of the negro who waited to take his
horse.

"See'd who, marsa?" asked Cesar in
return; the whites of his eyes dilating to
their utmost, meanwhile, in terrified surprise.

" 'See'd · who?' why, you rascal, the
gentleman who this moment came up to the
gate with me."

" Lor-a-mercy!" exclaimed the astonished

Cesar, "I did n't see notting at all, marsa! Golly! he must abin yer shadder."

"Well, say nothing about it, Cesar," returned the elder; "but put away the horse, and give him a good feed, for he has been out the best part of the day without anything.".

The matter, however, was fated not to be hushed up so easily; it chanced that Dorothy had been looking out the door at that moment, and had overheard the short passages between the negro and his master. She, therefore, on his coming into the house, plied the elder with question on question as to what such inquiries could mean. The elder tried to satisfy her—as men are wont to do when their ribs are troublesomely inquisitive—by fabricating various little fibs, &c. But Dorothy was not to be thus put off; she menaced him with hysterics, fainting-fits, and the like, to the end of her days, if he would not tell her the honest truth about it; till at length poor Tub was compelled to purchase his peace by making a clean breast about the matter.

But his troubles ended not even then; for

Dorothy insisted upon an immediate visit to parson Smearsoul, late as it then was, in order that the whole business might be submitted to his judgment. However, as, on reflection, it was deemed easier to have the parson come, than for them to go, Cesar was despatched forthwith upon that important errand.

CONCLUDING CHAPTER.

Wherein is satisfactorily cleared up all that hath puzzled the reader in the foregoing part of the narrative. Moreover, all the personages brought to view in this authentic history are herein disposed of, in a way at which it is hoped the good nature of the reader will take no offence.

ACCOMPANIED by his reverend brother Spume, at half-past eleven of the clock, *past meridian*, arrived at our hero's domicile the Rev. Mr. Smearsoul. The amiable Keziah had for some reason arisen, and was found by the reverend visitants seated at a stand, with the family Bible before her, and interestingly attired in a light loose robe, which threw an air of grace about her person.

The several appearances of Paddle were described, and his several communications rehearsed, to the reverend gentleman. Great was their astonishment thereat—many were

11*

their ejaculations of pious horror—many the
upturnings of their eyes.   Occasionally,
indeed, and when they thought the eyes of
the family were off of them, the two divines
would exchange knowing and humorous
glances, while the goblin's more striking
and ludicrous passages were being recited.
But this was between themselves; to the
others they expressed a holy horror at the
. whole affair.

"I should strongly incline, elder Tub,"
said Parson Smearsoul, when the elder had
finished his narrative, " to resolve this affair
into a demoniacal visitation—for why should
not demons now manifest themselves as
well as formerly?—but in the last of the
supposed appearances a horse, as well as a
man, was visible to you.   Now, as horses
have no souls, there can be no spiritual
embodiments in that form.   Consequently"———

Here the Rev. Mr. Spume begged leave to
interpose a question.   He begged his reverend brother to remember that some devils
entered into a herd of hogs in the days
of the Saviour—" Might not a devil have

been in the horse which the goblin **Paddle** bestrode?"

"Nay, brother," answered Mr. Smear-soul, "for the devil in the swine destroyed not their visibility; whereas the horse in question, though visible to the elder, was not so to the negro Cesar.

"Consequently, Mr. Tub," resumed the Parson, from where brother Spume had broken him off, "my conclusion is that the appearances were illusory; and that the supposed communications were suggested by your own carnal reason. There is a class of heretics who have lately manifested themselves hereabout, Mr. Tub, whose doctrine is that all are to be finally saved, without reference to their deeds or characters in this life. To some persons of that class, I fear, you have at one time and another listened, and your mind has become tinctured with their blasphemous and presumptuous reasonings.

"This, elder Tub, to my mind, fully explains the whole matter before us. You have harbored those evil suggestions until your imagination, being excited thereby, has conjured up the phantasm of the goblin Paddle, and made it to seem to speak what, in reality, was conceived and brought forth by your own depraved reason.

"Elder Tub, this must not be longer borne with; when the church was weak in number and means, she was necessitated to be more lenient toward offending members than strictly comported with her obligations to her great head. But now, elder Tub, that our numbers are greatly increased, we must begin to lop off the dry and profitless branches.

"Besides, elder Tub, you have been less liberal of your carnal substance to the church, than your circumstances would warrant. In relation to that substance you are but God's steward, Mr. Tub, and you are robbing him when you withhold what he demands of it for carrying on his work of grace in the world. Think of these things, elder Tub," continued the parson, sententiously, as he rose to depart, "and may Heaven grant you grace, that you may, through his instrument the church, be disposed to render unto God the things that are God's.——Good-night, Mr. Tub."

"You understand managing that old chap, I perceive, brother Smearsoul," remarked Asaph Spume, as arm in arm the two reverend gentlemen trudged homeward together; "you are safe for a doubling of his subscription for the ensuing year, at least, and I should not be surprised if he sent you a good round present, by way of a preliminary peace-offering, ere to-morrow's sun goes down. The old fellow, I take it, has pretty well lined his pouch from those broad flats of his."

"Yes, and from a long course of dealing in his store which borders as closely on the nefarious as the law will allow," answered Mr. Smearsoul. "There are but two things which prevent his being a rogue outright within the widest limits of the law; those are, a fear of losing his custom by being turned out of church; and a fear of being endlessly damned in the future life. I find that, among my male members, it is only the baser and more ignorant class that I can affect by the latter consideration. By the way Keziah Tub—you noticed her—did you not? She is a saint—the salt of the family—and would make a good wife, no doubt."

"And whoever gets her will get spoons with her—heigh?" laughingly put in the pious Asaph. "Ah, ah! brother Smear-soul—she is the salt of the family, is she? and you think of pickling yourself in that barrel? Pretty good—pretty good, brother Smearsoul." Thus sported the two parsons.

The Tub family, meanwhile, repaired to bed, but not—so far as respects the elder and Dorothy—to sleep. On the contrary, they lay awake the livelong night, engaged in active diplomatic scheming and contriving.

"It would be inconvenient to be turned out of church now," concluded the elder, for the late revival has very considerably increased its members, and I shall have nearly all thar custom at my store if I retain my standing."

"And besides that," put in Dorothy, "our Keziah is getting well along in years, and ought to be married if she is ever going to be. Mr. Smearsoul has a high opinion of her piety, and praises her gift in prayer. It would help our influence mightily if a match could be made between them."

"And another thing," added the elder, " people are taking on mightily now-a-days about temperance. I have been urged to sign the pledge several times of late, and have promised to do so when I have sold out my present stock of liquors. Deacon Splawfoot, too, has been compelled to stop his distillery. Now I can manage, by watering them pretty freely, to make my liquors hold out for a considerable time, and they will bring a better price now that the deacon's distillery is stopt."

Well, the result arrived at by the pious old couple was, that the elder should visit parson Smearsoul early next morning—confess to him his mental backslidings—lay the whole blame thereof upon the devil—profess a greater horror of heresy than he had ever experienced before—double his subscription for the parson's salary—and enjoin on parson Smearsoul the obligation of secrecy relative to the whole business.*

* This may account why the people about there are

"And," added the provident Dorothy, "it will be as well when you start fer thar, to have Cesar put a bag of apples into the wagon, and a bushel or two of corn, for a present to Mr. Smearsoul."

It remains but to be added, reader, that in all these worldly-wise calculations our hero sped to admiration. He was retained in his ecclesiastical standing and dignity. His liquors held out to admiration. The taint of heresy never afterward attached to him, for, aware of his vulnerability to suspicion on that score, he goes the 'whole animal' in the opposite direction. He therefore has nearly the whole run of church custom; and, what goes still more to enlarge and strengthen his influence to that effect, is, that she who was once Miss Keziah Tub, is now Mrs. Smearsoul.

As to the impious goblin Paddle, he has never since been seen in the parts, either on foot or on horseback; and devoutly is it to be wished that he never will.

not informed of the facts of this history, which is now, for the first time, given to the public.

APPENDIX

TO THE FOREGOING NARRATIVE.

THE foregoing narrative, gentle reader, is in a lighter and more ludicrous strain than it suits the author's general taste to write, or yours, it may be, to peruse; if you have supposed his design therein to have been mere amusement, at the expense of opinions and usages held sacred by many, you have greatly misconceived it. An author, as well as a public speaker, finds that different modes of address must be resorted to, in order to gain access to different minds. Some may be reached by closely reasoned argumentation—some would prefer to have the argument diluted with some florid and gratuitous declamation—some require to be stung into reflection with sarcasm—and some with playful satire. In this case, the design has been to bring before the mind some facts connected with the notion of endless misery, which are not generally taken into the account when that topic is under consideration; but which, on account of their magnitude, are worthy of a place in the serious thoughts of all; and if the undeniable results of a doctrine are to have any bearing on the decision as to its truth or fal-

12

sity, then ought those herein exhibited to seal the
fate of the dogma of endless woe, effectually and forever.

The suggestions respecting the magnitude of hell,
and the kind of inhabitants which (among others) it
must contain, are all, as the author conceives, fully
within the range of probability, and might have been
carried even considerably farther; the intelligent reader,
on reflection, cannot but entirely concur in this.   The
Rev. Dr. Wilson, of Albany, apparently a very con-
scientious Presbyterian clergyman, published a sermon
a few years since, in which he asserts that the majority
of the framers of our federal constitution were deists or
atheists.   The great and good Washington, himself,
he supposes to have held the Christian religion in light
esteem; the faith of Jefferson, Madison, Monroe and
Franklin, he considers to have been more than doubtful; and that of the Adamses' (being Unitarianism) is,
in his judgment, but little better; nor is Dr. Wilson
alone, by a great deal, in these suppositions.   It is
presumed that very, *very* few orthodox ministers can
be found who would deliberately affirm, that they believe these distinguished personages to have possessed
that pure faith, and to have undergone that divine experience, which are held to be indispensable to salvation; and if they did not, then, on the popular hypothesis of endless misery, they are all damned!

As to the distinguished personages of antiquity, the
author has allowed the goblin to allot a place in hell to
only such of them, as, from their histories, are undoubtedly there, on the endless misery hypothesis.

Marcus Junius Brutus, with all his virtues, (and by universal testimony these were many and eminent,) terminated his life by suicide—which was a common case in those days. The virtuous Roman matron, who did the same to resent her violation, and thereby occasioned the first overthrow of monarchical power of which history furnishes the record, must be consigned to a common hell with the infamous Cleopatra! It were vain to enlarge, however, for the scope for this kind of reflections is boundless. The author here but just touches on these facts, that the reader may see that our veritable friend Paddle's speculations about hell and its inhabitants, are not absolutely gratuitous; in fact, they were entirely designed as an indirect mode of argumentation, and couched in their present form the better to secure a reading and awaken reflection

It is hoped that the serious and moderate portion of his orthodox readers, will not accuse the author of an attempt to ridicule *their* professions or practice in the person of Elder Tub. It is known that hypocrites and double-minded persons are to be found amongst all religious classes—Christian, Jew, Mahomedan, and Pagan; against pretenders of this class only are the shafts of his ridicule directed. The sincere Christian has his respect and his affection, wherever, or of what denomination soever, he is found.

> "To those he renders more than mere respect,
> Whose actions say that they respect themselves."

But the hypocrite has his detestation and contempt, whether he be orthodox or heterodox; for neither the one nor the other is free from his intrusions, according as he judges that with the one or the other his selfish ends may be best promoted.

The reader may be curious to know whether there is actually such a spot on the Virginia shore of the Ohio as that described in the preceding narrative. To this the author can only answer, that he was informed some years ago that there is a stone on that shore, the precise *locale* of which he did not learn, which bears an inscription to the purport of the one described. This is all he knows about it; the rest is fancy.

THE

OLD MAN OF THE HILL-SIDE.

12*

THE

OLD MAN OF THE HILL-SIDE.

A TALE.

Of which the reader has the author's permission to believe
all that may strike him as true, and to reject the remainder.

ıᴛ were, perhaps, superfluous to state
that the old man of the hill-side lives on
the side of a hill; for that much will be
likely to be inferred as a matter of course;
but it may not be amiss to describe him as
a queer old customer, because, as that does
not of necessity follow from his living on a
hill-side, the reader would not be apt to
know it except he were so informed.

He measures in height, does he of the
hill-side, just six feet as he stands, but when
stretched out as he will be when his under
taker has to do with him, his length wil

fall little short of six feet six. A piercing grey eye, and a nose which terminates in a sharp peak, give to his otherwise comical expression a character of shrewdness and penetration, which is amply corroborated by his usual remarks upon men and things.

Not overmuch reverence for the clergy has that same old man, nor backward is he in "spaakin' his mind till them," as he himself expresses it. Indeed, it must be owned that they find him a serious bore at times, for on no class of persons is he more prone to exercise his privilege of tongue than on them.

For example. The Rev. Simon Soft, having lately been delivered of a very towering sermon, was shortly afterward at an evening party, at which our hero was present, where he managed—the said Simon—after several ineffectual efforts, to make his big discourse the topic of conversation. Most of the party praised it highly—it was rich—it was splendid—and all that. Simon, however, affected to run it down; he wasn't quite well when he preached it; he had not studied it at all; had thrown it off hastily, and without much thought, etc., etc. "What is your opinion of it, my old friend?" inquired he at length of him of the hill-side. "I observed that you listened to it with great attention."

"Indaad thin," replied the old man, "and do ye think I'll be at the throuble to kaap in mind a discoorse that you say didn't cost you any mind at all, at all? Sure I kaap my head for a bether purpose nor that comes to."

"But," said Simon, sheepishly, and taken all aback by the old man's answer, "I don't think that my sermon was so *very* poor an one after all, notwithstanding that I bestowed so little thought upon it. Some minds are so constituted," continued the modest Simon, "as to be capable of brilliant efforts with little previous preparation; and as to that discourse of mine, the generality of my hearers admired it very much."

"Troth, thin, and big fools weer they for that same," retorted our hero; "an I knoud whin ye weer rinnin' it down, that it was fishin' for praise ye weer, but I'm not such a gudgeon as to bite at a hook so poorly kivered. Hout man! whin it happens til ye to praach better than ordiner, the paaple will find it out, and ye've no naad to be pumpin at thim for compliments to fill yer vanity wid."

So much for Simon's out-come with the old man of the hill-side. Too many preachers there are, it must be owned, of the Simon Soft family, who, when they believe themselves to have performed better than usual, must needs leak out their vanity by a similar fishing for compliments.

I took a walk to the old man's cabin on the hill-side one Monday morning, in company with a young clergyman who had preached for us the day before, whose manners and speech gave evidence that he cherished a towering opinion of his own abilities. His style in the desk had been marked by a stiffness and pomposity which I knew could not have escaped, my old friend's notice, for I had occasionally cast my eye toward where he sat, and could easily divine from the uneasy twinkling of his eye, and his frequent change of position, that the foppery of the young preacher was

not at all to his taste. And, to confess the
truth, it was for the sake of the lesson
which I knew the old man would not fail to
administer to him, that I had prevailed on
him to accompany me to his cabin.

I had conjectured rightly, for scarcely had
we been ten minutes seated ere the old man
began to criticise my companion's pronun-
ciation of certain words—those, especially,
in which the *r* occurred—and to quiz him
in respect to his pompous verbiage. In his
prayer, for instance, the young man had
invoked the Lord to *come down in his char-
iot of light.* "Did ye mane by that same,"
enquired the old man, "that the Lord
should ride down through the ruf of the
maatin'-house in his coach?" The young
preacher reddened to his ears with vexation
and perplexity, for, in truth, he had attached
no particular meaning to that petition when
he made it.

"And why dount ye," continued the old
man, "whin ye mane *brithrin,* say *brithrin,*
at once? Sure there's no naad of sayin'
ber-rith-erin. And why dount ye say *Christian frinds?* for divil a bit of naadcissity

is there for sayin' *Cur-ristian fur-rinds.*
And thin, at the commincement, sure ye
make a naadless pother of words; ye say,
' *Bur-rith-erin, we will inter-o-duce the high
praises of our-er God, in the use of the sub-
lime and delightful stanzas, recor-r-ded on
the one hundred and thir-r-tieth page.'*
Hout man! what can be the maanin' of all
that bur-r-r-rin? Sure bigger praachers nor
you git along wid less kalaver. Takin' yer
high-soundin' discourse togither wid the
little sinse belongin' till it, made me concaat
that I was on a staamboat that had too
much staam in its boilers."

This was rather a cool cloud for my
young friend to come in contact with in his
flight toward the sun; yet I was quite easy
on the score of its depressing him to his
hurt, for he was of that class of geniuses
whose self-esteem leads them to set a very
low estimate on the judgments of those who
fail to recognize their preëminent merits.
Accordingly, as we were returning together
he remarked to me, "That's a very con-
ceited old man; he has a wretched taste in
respect to matters of language and preach-

ing; he is the first man that ever *faulted* me on those grounds." Proof positive of his bad taste, thought I.

"Arrah now, are ye sure it isn't invious ye are?" asked the old man of the hill-side of a Rev. Mr. Twiddle, who was nibbling, in a spirit of hyper-criticism, at a discourse delivered in this desk by a stranger on the previous Sabbath, and with which the whole audience besides were highly delighted.

"Sure the bist tist of a good sermon," continued the old man, "is to find the paaple plaised wid it—for wud ye not pronounce a puddin' good when all the aiters of it weer plaised wid its taste? Troth wud ye, man. And what if somebody that pretinded to be a judge of cookery shuld say, that it wasn't mixed and boiled accordin' to rule. Why, man, wud ye care a ha'porth about that if yer mout was shuted? Divil a bit wud ye. So take an ould man's counsel, Musther Twiddle, and niver spaak agin a discoorse when iverybody ilse is shuted wid it; for paaple will suspicion ilse, that

13

it's jealous ye are that the praacher is betther liked nor yersilf."

The old man of the hill-side, however, is
not always thus cynical in his tone toward
clergymen; I have sometimes heard him
address them in terms of patronizing encour-
agement; but when he does so, it is because
he perceives that a strain of that sort is
required by the diffidence of the party; and
he has a surprisingly quick and accurate
discernment in such matters.

A modest, and really talented young man,
had for three or four years preached to the
society of which the old man is a member;
he exchanged desks one Sabbath with a
neighboring clergyman who does not possess
one half of his abilities, but who, when he
ministers in a strange place, is in the habit
of dragging into his discourse all the pretty
and sparkling ideas of which he is in
possession; and this, to persons who hear
him but seldom, gives him the appearance
of being a very splendid and interesting
preacher.

Consequently, when my modest friend
returned to his parish, he could hear little

else than the praises of the stranger with whom he had exchanged. Never had so great a sermon been delivered from that pulpit—*he* was the man—they had never heard a preacher to compare with him—if they could but get *him* settled among them they would be quite made up—&c., &c.

My young friend began to feel seriously discouraged; he was not envious—modest men seldom are—but his natural diffidence increased upon him on a comparison of the high compliments bestowed on the stranger with the faint ones expressed towards him- self. Moreover, he had heard one of his regular hearers say, that he would rather part with his best cow than that the ser- vices of so splendid a preacher should fail of being permanently engaged by the con- gregation.

" A fig's ind !" indignantly exclaimed the old man of the hill-side, when my modest friend had hinted his discouragement to him. " Why, havn't I been over into the stranger's parish sin Sunda? And aren't the paaple theer as much plaazed wid you as some of uz weer wid him ? In troth are they man; and glad enoof wud they be to take ye in lieu of him if they culd git ye. But the sinsible part of uz wudn't be such fools as to listen til it, nor the semple part naather, whin once they've come back til theer sinses.

"So take heart, man, take heart," continued the old man, "yerself was a new toy wid uz once, and tickled enoof weer we all wid you thin; but now we've worn some of the paint and gildin' aff of ye, and some maybe wud be willin' to barter ye for a frish bauble. But I wudn't, man, and they that wud, wud soon be sick of that same. As to the chap that says he wud give his best cow for the ixchange, he has niver given the value of a cow's tail toward supportin' any preachin' yit; nor will he till cow's tails get to be plintier than promises wid him, and that's not soon, I'll warrant ye."

The old man of the hill-side was not wide of the mark in his views upon these heads. People are fond of new things, and it often happens that a new, though inferior preacher, will extract more compliments from them than will older ones of **great and** acknowledged ability.

Nevertheless, I have known preachers, not a few, who were silly-pated enough to allow their vanity to be inflated by that sort of incense. On the part of very young men, who have not had experience enough to acquaint them with the utter worthlessness of such flatteries, some weakness of the sort may be allowed; but a preacher of several years' experience in such matters, who, when told that at such a place he out-preached all the preaching that had ever been heard there, jumps to the self-satisfy-ing conclusion that, therefore, he is a man of superior abilities to the best of those who had previously ministered at that place—such a preacher, I say, may be set down as an incorrigible coxcomb. Good faith, his brains might, without much detriment to their thinking qualities, be exchanged for an equal bulk of buttermilk.

13*

Adjacent to our old friend's farm there is a wild and uninhabited tract of country, of five or six miles in breadth, through which the paths are so narrow and indistinct that the traveller must pick his way by means of what is termed in the parts a *blaize* or *marking*, on the trunks of trees; and as these intersect each other in various directions, it is necessary that he should well know the bearings of the point for which he is aiming, and keep a sharp look-out into the bargain.

It is on the very edge of this forest that the old man's farm is situated; and many a sheep has he lost by the predatory propensities of his neighbors the wolves; his hen-roosts, too, could tell many a tale of nightly invasion by those bushy-tailed rogues, which, from time immemorial, have rivalled even Methodist preachers in their tender affection for all sorts of poultry; and often, moreover, have the deer of that forest so well grazed the old man's fields of winter grain as to have materially lessened his labor of reaping them.

I was sitting with him in his porch one beautiful spring morning, when, pointing my attention to a field of young oats, on which I perceived a large doe, and two fawns to be quietly trespassing, he laughed heartily at the sense of security they manifested, as if conscious that' he was unfurnished with the means of resenting their intrusion. "Arrah, now!" exclaimed the old man, "isn't it a mortal shame that it's niver a dog nor gun I have, to táche those bastes bether manners nor to rob an ould man like me of his hard-earned crops? Faix, if they would go over till my next necbor's, and try the same wid him, he would be soon sinding a rifle-ball afther thim to tache thim what's dacent."

Two preachers rode up to the old man's domicile one day, who informed him that they were on their way to a quarterly meeting, which was to commence that evening in the settlement next adjoining, and they solicited the old man's guidance through the intermediate woods, as a recent *wind-fall* had rendered the track more obscure than usual. They were both of them sleek-looking men, and were mounted on sleek-looking horses; their plump and self-satisfied countenances indicated that they were in possession of the godliness which, at the least, is profitable for the life that now is.

One of them was a presiding elder, and as he must needs be present to open the meeting aforesaid, he urged this as a motive for prompt compliance on the part of our old friend. After a few shrewd glances at these plump ecclesiastics, the old man quietly assumed his hat and staff, and trudged on in advance of the travellers.

It was a desperate path; now almost impassable to horses on account of the huge hemlock roots, which extended and interlaced over the entire surface of the ground; now by rocks, which nearly hid the soil for many contiguous acres; and now by a vegetable muck—converted into mire by the humidity of the air in that overshadowing forest, which, from its density, excluded the exhaling warmth of the sun.

After plodding on in silence for two or three miles the old man made a sudden halt, and, addressing himself to the elder, said. "Come now, my fine fillow, you have a stouter pair of ligs nor me, suppose you give thim a little natheral ixercise in the way of walkin, and let me bestride your baste for a bit."

The elder was utterly astounded at the cool impudence of this proposition. "What, *I* walk!" he exclaimed; "I can consent to no such thing, sir; by any means; I am unused to walking, sir; and, besides sir, it is not the usage to which I am accustomed, sir; *some* respect is due to my office, sir; for I am about God's business, and woe betide the man who attempts to obstruct it, sir."

"Och, what a botheration ye make now," retorted our hero, "because ye 're axed to take a little ixercise in the natheral way. And is it bether than me ye are because ye 're a praacher? Faix, and it 's myself that dount agree wid ye in that same; and the divil a peg furder will I gow wid ye, my fine fillow, uiiliss ye lend me the back of yer baste for that purpose. So now ye may take yer choice."

The poor elder was now in a quandary,

sure enough; he found he had got into the hands of a crooked Christian; to pick his own way through the remaining part of the forest he saw to be clearly impossible; the old man's guidance he *must* have, on such terms as he could. On the other hand, the alternative of footing it amongst rocks, and roots, and mire, was a hard one, and scarcely preferable to his taking his chance of getting lost. He therefore softened his tone toward the old man—plead that walking would exhaust his strength and unfit him for preaching—that it would bespatter his garments, which were new and glossy, and bemire his boots, which had been polished for the occasion.

But all would not do; our old friend was inexorable. " Hout man," said he, " sure ye'll have as claan a fut as I will, or, for the mather of that, as claan a fut as there'll be at the maatin, for few are they that will ride theer. And faix theer's no use in chaffering heer thegither, for if ye dount lind me yer baste, I dount go a peg furder wid ye."

The elder was fain to submit at length which he did with the worst grace possible remarking at the same time, that as he couldn't walk more than a mile at the utmost, he should expect his horse yielded back to him as soon as he required it.

"Will, I'm agraad to that," said our friend of the hill-side, "or to anythin' ilse that's raisonable. But ye must spaak out loud, do ye mind, for I'm dull of haarin' whin I git on the back of a baste—the ixercise is new til me."

The sequel proved our hero correct as to his dulness of hearing; for, after floundering among rocks and mire for a half a mile or so, the elder complained of being out of breath, and requested the old man to stop—but the latter gave no signs of hearing. The elder raised his voice higher, and higher still, until it reached a bawl—still our friend's deafness was as invincible as before. The elder quickened his pace to a half run, in the hope of getting nearer to his troublesome guide; but, from some unaccountable cause, the horse on which the latter was mounted increased his gait in the same ratio.

And thus things continued, until, at the end of three miles or so, they emerged from

the forest into the open country where the
old man's services ceased to be necessary.
He therefore came to a halt, dismounted,
and waited for the coming up of the elder,
who was blowing like a porpoise, his round
countenance as red as the sun in smoke
days, and his sacred person most sadly be-
spattered from head to heels.

" Look ye theer now," said our friend of
the hill-side, in a serio-comic tone, "what a
dacent color ye have afther yer walk. Sure
I know'd a little natheral exercise wud
improve yer health. But ye carry too much
burthen of hardweer about ye, man, for ye
have a spur on ivery fut of ye, which
incumbered yer walkin', or ilse ye'd have
performed yer part bether nor one of the
king's fut guards. As for yer boots, the
divil a testher of harm wull the mud do
thim whin once they get use till it; for
havn't I taken many such a walk? Faix
have I, and my brogans dount know the
differ betwixt bein' clane or dirthy. It's
good for ye, man, to faal some of the throu-
bles of life, for thin ye can spake til the paaple from yer own ixparience."

The poor elder, during this parting lecture, was inflated with indignation nearly to bursting; he had sense enough remaining, however, to perceive that its explosion upon the old man of the hill-side would be but so much breath thrown away, in addition to what he had already lost in the three-mile chase in which he had been engaged. He therefore stifled it as best he could, and proceeded on to meet his expectant congregation, possibly to edify them with a discourse on the Christian graces of meekness and humility.

It must not be inferred that the old man of the hill-side is an indifferentist in respect to religion; much less that he is unbelieving. He is neither, by any means. He is, indeed, a contemner of its mere ceremonial, and of extra, or ostentatious pretensions to sanctity on the part of its professors. He holds at a

14

cheap rate upturned eyes, and such pious
ejaculations as seem—and *all* so seem when
publicly indulged in—more meant for man's
ear than for God's.   The class of our hero's
acquaintances whose piety oozes out in such
forms, have a great dread of his waggery,
which he exercises on them without stint
when he chances to be in that vein, and that
is not seldom.

A countryman of his whom he had long
known very intimately, and who was much
more given to public exhibitions of piety
than to the practice of righteousness in his
everyday intercourse, was accompanying
our old friend at one time in an excursion to
a distant market-town.   They tarried over
night at an inn, in a single room of which
nearly a score of persons, including themselves, were put to lodge. These were mostly
travellers bound to the same market-town,
and on a similar errand with their own.

"Why, hout, Robin!" exclaimed the old
man to his companion, whom, on his return
from the stable, whither he had been at-
tending to the comfort of his horses, he
found kneeling at his bedside near the door

of the crowded apartment aforesaid, amid a perfect confusion of talking, smoking, passing in and out, and other noises incident to such an occasion. "Why, hout, man! is it yerself ye'er mutherin to down theer? Or is it to the infinite Baaing who can listen til the heart when it spaaks, though the mout be silent? Fie on ye, Robin, and git ye up out of this, for ye'll git the ligs of ye thrampled aff by some of the heavy-futted gintlemin passin' in and out. And as for yer preers, man, I'm thinkin' the Almighty dount naad thim so badly that ye must be pattherin' thim over til him amidst all this clishmaclaver."

When his companion had arisen and was stripping for bed, the old man continued his well-meant raillery at his servile adherence to the mere externals of piety, to the neglect of its loving spirit and beneficent practice; but he softened his voice to a more conciliatory tone.

"And sure now, Robin," said he, "I didn't know but ye maybe had gone to carry a saddle of vinison, or a few rolls of butther, or some iggs, or somethin' of the

soort which we can well speer between uz,
til the poor family near by that weer �: urnt
out yesthernight.   Sure, Robin, those poor
paaple naad hilp more nor the Lord naads
preers.   And its pricious little good all our
pathor nosthors will do uz, I'm thinkin',
ixcipt they pit grace intil our hearts to move
us to hilp the poor and the naady.   So
think of it, Robin, and if it's of any use til
ye yer religion is, lit the same be manifist
in yer daads of charity to the sufferin', and
of kindness and uprightness toward yer
neebors."

There was another individual in the parts,
on whom our old man of the hill-side was
as prone to exercise his privilege of blunt
counsel as on his friend Robin, and for a
similar reason.

This was a tall, lank store-keeper, whose
pretensions were of the very saintliest sort.
He wore a buttonless and collarless coat,
and as nearly seamless also as he could
have it.   His hair, which was long and
silken, he wore parted in the middle of the
forehead, and flowing down on his shoul-
ders like in the pictures of the Saviour.

His words were honeyed, his step stealthy, his conversation plentifully interlarded with saintly sighs. So soon as he entered a place of worship, down he dropt on his knees with his long body prostrated upon a bench, and his head overspread by his handkerchief as with a pall; and thus would he lie, groaning and sobbing, during the entire services of the meeting. Nevertheless, if this embodiment of sanctity was not more than a little knavish in his dealings, then was he most grievously belied by his neighbors of every kind.

Our friend of the hill-side knew him "like a book," and on entering a meeting once where he was prostrated as described, he took him to task in his own blunt way for having left his horse exposed in the broiling sun, when there was the shelter of a woods within the distance of a few rods, where others of the congregation had tied their horses.

"And sure, Musther Melden," said he, "but ye do ill to be slobbering heer, wuth all these paaple to wutniss the ado ye're makin' about religion, while yer poor baste

14*

stands out theer all the while, wid the flies
aatin' him, and no shilther agin the haat of
the sun.   Troth, man, the Baaing ye profess
to be prayin' to made the four-futted crather
out theer as well as yersilf, and it's some
tinder regard for it ye should have for that
same raason, if no ither.

"And dount the Scripture say, Musther
Melden, that the merciful man is merciful
til his baast?   But sure it's little mercy
theer is in laavin' it to be devoured wid
flies.   So git ye up, man; for if they are
matthers betwaan you and God ye are
waapin about, ye have maybe a closet at
home wheer ye can waap in sacret, which
wull be more dacent nor to be makin' a
shew of yer graaf before all these paaple.
And it's little, man, that the great Creathor
cares about the posthure of yer body, that
ye must naads sprawl yersilf on the flure at
this unraasonable rate.   He looks at the
soul, man, and requires that we should be
merciful as he is merciful."

It is a distinguished and pleasing trait in
our old friend's character, blunt as he is in
speech, and hard in feature, that he has a

neart big with humanity toward all living creatures. He decidedly objects to the killing of birds and squirrels, and all creatures whose existence is not incompatible with human safety.

"For murther is bad spoort, if spoort be the object," he says; "and if it be done for the aatin's sake, sure it's none but a gluttonous baaste that wud sacrifice the mirry and joyous life of a little bird for a maar moutful of dainty maat."

We were driving together in a dearborn up a rugged acclivity one day, when we were startled by the well-known, melancholy, tremulous note of a rattlesnake, which was under the very feet of the horse, who, however, being a quietly disposed animal, stept cautiously over the reptile without evincing much excitement. When we had proceeded on a few steps I stopt the horse, and, getting out of the vehicle, took up a large stick with the purpose of killing the snake, which by that time had got on to a stump on the other side of the road, and lay coiled there.

"Sorra a bit of harm shall ye do the

craather," said the old man. "Is it aavil for good ye wud do til it, and so prove yersilf a woorse Christian nor the snake? Sure it was kind of the craather not to bite the lig of yer horse whin theer was danger of itself bein' thrampled on, and since it has allowed ye to pass unharmed it wud be an ill part of ye to kill it in return. Lit it leve, theer's room enough in these wuds for all of uz."

The old man's logic prevailed, and the rattlesnake went free, nor have I ever since regretted, but rather have rejoiced at the lenient decision which balanced accounts of obligation between the reptile and me.

"I was ridin' out of a city for a bit of an ixcursion," said he, in a conversation we once had together at his residence, "on a plissant Sathurday afthernoon, whin I was overtaken by a praacher who was goin' into the counthry to hould a maatin on the morrow. So we jogged on thegither; and he had a daal to say fornent the importance of gittin' religion and savin' the immorthal soul. Well, by and by we mit a man wuth a wagon-load of shaap that he was takin' in to be slaughthered. The wither was hot and drauthy, and the poor crathers weer pantin' with haat and thirst. So, as he stopt at a pump to git himsilf a dthrink, I axed him to give the shaap a dthrink too.

" ' Nonsinse,' ixclaimed the riverind man at my side, ' he is takin' thim in to be killed to-night for Monday's market, and a dthrink will be of no use til thim, only for a little while.'

" ' Faix, thin, yer riverince,' said I, ' if yersilf weer goin' to be slaughthered to-night, or if ye weer on yer dyin' bid, wud ye think, whin the thirst of death was on ye, that it was naadliss to haad yer supplications for wather for yer parched mout, because it's so little time ye'd faal the good of it? Troth wud ye not, man; but ye'd crave God's blissin' on the hand that raached it til ye. Sorra a bit wud ye think it naadliss thin.'

" It was ivident that the man wuth the shaap (who overheard me) filt the force of this appaal, for widout more ado he wathered his shaap all round, and, och, it ached the heart of me to see how graathily

the poor crathers dthrunk it down, and
how they licked the hands of the man in
saamin' gratitude for the favor.

"Well, as the riverind man and I rode on
thegither, he tould me that for the futhure I
wud do bether to attind til my own affeers,
and not throuble mysilf about the sufferins
of dumb animals. 'Bear your own throu-
bles, ould gintleman,' said he, 'and lave
ithers to bear theer's as they can.'

"'The de'il be in me if I wull,' answered
I, [and the old man here straightened himself to his full measure of six feet six.]
'And is it yersilf that wud be axin me to do
it? and you a praacher of that religion that
taaches mercy and tinderness! Och, thin,
I pity the paaple who have the likes of ye
for a laader; and it's a thousand times
bether stay at home ye had, than to go
about taachin' yer own silfishness til the
paaple, whin, the Lord knows, they've no
lack of it widout ye.

"'Why, man,' continued I, 'if we lived
neebors, and my dog, in my absence, wud
sometimes stand at yer table, lickin' his
chaps for a moutful of maat, and ye wud

giv it til him, I wud faal the obligation as if the same were done til mysilf. Well, thin, the birds and bastes are all God's craathers; he shews his concern for thim in providin' for theer faadin and coverin; but some of thim he has lift til our care, because he has subjected thim more ispecially til our use. But the right to *use*, does not imply the right to *abuse* thim—no, nor to *niglict* thim naather—and himsilf will be theer avinger, man, upon those who do thim wrong in any manner. So good bye, and a tinderer heart til ye.' "

'There prevailed, during one of my sojourns in the old man's neighborhood, a more than ordinary ado about religion; almost everybody in the parts seemed infected by it; night after night, be the weather what it would, people came together from considerable distances, and until ten, eleven, and even twelve o'clock, they would sing, pray, exhort, and relate experiences. That a majority of the actors in such scenes are sincere for the time, perhaps, it were uncharitable to doubt. Nevertheless, to affirm that pure and undefiled

religion is concerned in exhibitions so dis-
cordant, and so revolting to the cultivated
moral sense, would be to pay her an unmer-
itedly low compliment, methinks.

Truth is, there is scarcely a rural neighborhood throughout our country that has
not, at one time, or another, been the
scene of that sort of epidemic; and if but
a tithe of the folks were really Christians, that are reported to have been so
made at such times, then, in sooth, would
we be quite a Christian nation; and the
wonder then would be, how, by means so
repugnant to reason and the moral sense,
religion could accomplish results so salu-
tary.

" Havn't you *a word* to say for Jesus, old
man ?" asked a leader of one of these meet-
ings one evening, when all except our old
friend of the hill-side had rendered in their
experiences—perhaps for the fiftieth time
during the reigning excitement. The leader
aforesaid was somewhat of a stranger to our
old friend, being from another settlement
some two or three townships removed. "A

sinner at your time of life," continued he, "and not *one word* to say for Jesus!"

"Why, thin," was the characteristic reply, "if spaakin' for him's all that's naadful to hilp on his cause, faix, words are chaap, and they cost me no more nor the rist of ye. But, belikes, Jaasus is not a ha'porth the bether for all yer exparience-tillin afther all; and if *he* is n't, sure I know of nobody ilse that is. Maybe if ye wud imitate him by goin' about doin' good—maybe if ye wud be maak and gintle, and tinder-hearted—visitin' the fatherless and widder in theer affliction, and kaapin yerselves unspotted from the world —maybe that wud be more til the purpose, and be a bether proof of yeer baain the disciples of Jaasus than all yer *words* will amount to.

"Och, frinds, and have n't I listened til ye for siveral avenins thegither, and have I heard iver a syllable from ye fornent the doin til ithers what ye wud that ithers shud do til you? Have I heard one of ye ax pardon of ithers for wrongs ye have done them in past life? Has a single mither's son of ye all, who may have defrauded yer neebors in times gone by, offered to make aminds til thim for the same? Sorra a thing of the kind have I wutnessed No; but ivery mither's son and daughter of ye says, 'I am determined to save my precious sowl,' —'I am hivven bint and hivven bound,'—'I faal that I have a title claar to mansions in the sky,' and the like; as if it was servin' God ye weer by maarly lookin' to yer own interests.

"Sure, frinds, it's altogether selfish yer religion is—it binifits none but yersilves, if it does that. Glad wud I be to join ye in a religion that wud promote paace and britherly love aming us—that wud laad us to saak truth, and timperance, and honest daalin wid each ither, and neeborly sociability, and the like virtues. But as to saving the immorthal sowl, I lave that to him who alone can do it. I have no faars that the God who gave my spirit til me will fail to take care of it. My concern, frinds, is to live well for the prisint—the futhur I lave wuth him."

To the afore-mentioned leader of the meeting these sentiments seemed as the sum of all error and impiety, boiled down to their quintessence. To the rest of the audience, however, who knew our friend better, they seemed but as the characteristic utterances of an honest heart, to which the every-day life of the speaker faithfully corresponded. For all agreed in regarding the old man of the hill-side as a man of blameless rectitude of character; but devoid, nevertheless, of the least spark of genuine religion.

———————

In one of my visits to our old hill-side acquaintance I drew from him a sketch of his early history; it was not entirely destitute of romantic interest, blunt and matter-of-fact as he is in character. I will give the sketch in our friend's own words, as it would lose nearly all its charm in a version of my own.

"I was maybe siventaan, or such mather, and the regiment of horse to which my

father belonged was quarthered in a little
saaport town in ould Ireland, whin I wint
to tell my cousin, Kate McFarland, that the
throop was ordhered away till Quaabic, in
North Ameriky, and I had come to take my
lave of her—perhaps foriver.

"I found her bare-futted, and saakin saa-
shills in the bed of a creek, that came in
and wint out wid the tide: the retraat of
tide lift its bed nearly dthry, and it was a
usual amusemint of the boys and girls of the
town to wade in at such times and saak
shills.

"Kate was but thirtaan thin; we had
always been viry close frinds; many is the
time we had rambled thegither over mid-
dows kivered wid butter-cups and daisies;
many a stroll along hedge-rows had we
taken, pickin haws and birries; and we had
bird-nested too, thegither, over oft—Och
poor little birdies! over often for you! But
it's ying and innocent we thin' weer, and
naather of uz could till why we so loved
aach ither's company. But whin we came
to the lave-takin'—whin I hurried away
wid few words to concaal my waapin'—and

whin, lookin' behint me afther a bit, I saw
Kate sittin' by hersilf undher a hidge, wid
the skirt of her frock up til her eyes—
och, thin, the heart of me! the heart of
me!

"Well, years passed. My father died at
Quaabic whin I was twinty; I was thin
livin wid a farmer on the St. Lawrence
river who traated me cruelly, and whin my
father was a month or so buried, I rin
away, and crossed over intil the United
States. I knew before that I had a cousin
in Philadilphy, none liss than Kate's own
brither, whose father and mither had both
died since he and I had left ould Ireland,
and sorra a word had I heard what had become of poor Kate whin thus lift an orphan
and alone in the world. Naad I till ye that
I made my way immediately to my cousin
in Philadilphy? Faix, ye 'll know as much
widout tillin'.

"But it's a weary distance betwaan
Canada and Philadilphy to a frindless and
pinnyless boy. I 'll not ache the heart of
ye by a datail of what I siffered on the
way. Whin pressed wid hunger, I wud big

15*

a day's imploymint; but I niver axed for
bread, nor for inything in charity. I was
full three months raachin New York at that
rate, and from theer I wint in a sloop to
Philadilphy at half price, doin' work for
the ither half.

"Och, but· my heart baat wid anxiety,
whin I came widin sight of the city; wheer-
about in it my cousin lived I did n't know;
I feared he maybe had moved away; or
had died; and many ither fancies came intil
my mind. Judge, thin, of my surprise and
plissure, whin, on steppin my fut on the
.wharf, the virry man I sought was the first
to maat my eye! I was not a moment in
graspin' his hand.

" 'Terrence McFarland!' said I, 'the
lang-ligged chap that addrisses ye, is yer
cousin Pathrick, ounly son of yer father's
brither, Friderick. It's minths he's been
on his way til ye, man. What say ye til
him? Wilcome, or no wilcome?'

" 'Och, a thousand times wilcome!' re-
sponded he; 'wilcome as May-day flowers,
man, or, for that mather, as the virry light
of hivven.' And he shuk my hand as

though he wud shake aff the shoulther of me.

"Forthwutts we wint til his dwillin', which was on Wather' straat; we enthered through his little shop, wheer he kipt groceries and provisions for sale; he pointed my attintion til the chaases, rolls of butther, herrins, smoked maat, barrels of biscuit, codfish, and the like. 'Does this look like starvin?' he axed. 'Divil a bit of it,' I answered. 'Well, thin, make yersilf asy on that score,' said he, 'and hilp me kaap this shop, on such terms as we wull sittle upon betwaan uz, until such time as ye can find a chance to do bether.' Thus was I at wince provided for.

"Of Terrence McFarland I learned, that his sisther Kate, afther the death of her parents, was taken in· and fosthered by a wealthy ould barristher of the town, who, as he had never been married, and had few connexions that he cared inythin' for, purposed to educate, and do for her as for a daughther. 'Och, thin,' thought I, 'it's far beyont me she wull faal hersilf now.' And so, by degraas, I taught mysilf to think

of her as a swaat draam of my early life—
a baam of sunshine in my youthful sky—a
sthray note from win of the harps of hivven trilling on the heart-cords of my boy-
hood. But now—lost to me foriver. And
many was the day of saacret graif, and
night of waapin, that I experienced on that
same account. Faix, ying man, if it's in
love ye've ever been, ye'll not naad tellin'
how tinder it makes the heart of ye.

"In 1819 the yillow faver prevailed in
the district of Philadilphy that included our
shop and residence, and aming the earliest
of its victims was my poor cousin Terrence.
Words would faably tell how I bemoaned
him; we had lived four years thegither wid
niver an angry thought or spaach betwaan
uz. Whin I bought this farm, I had his
body removed from the Potter's Faild,
where I was forced by the city authorities
to bury it, and it now lies aming the copse
of chisnuts in the far corner of my rye-faild,
yonder. Mine shall lie theer wid it in due
time.

"Well, it now behooved me to write to
my cousin Kate; for she was Terrence's

only heir. Maanwhile, evints had been workin' on that side the wather to drive her off til Amiraky.

"It saams her kind frind the barristher had for a cook a virry artful and schaamin crathur of a wuman; and her daughther (nearly Kate's age) was as wicked and sly as the mither. What shud they do, but make it up betwaan thim to make Kate belaive, that the paaple of the town suspicioned her of livin wid the barristher as his mistress!

"Poor Kate niver wince doubted that such was really the prevailin' suspicion—it struck her as a virry likely thing—and she took hersilf to task for not havin' anticipated such a result before. Her virtuous pride was aroused; she wud free hersilf from that suspicious position as soon as possible—that she wud.

"Consequintly, she seized the earliest opportunity of tellin' the barristher that circumstances demanded her prisence in Amiraky, and axin' his permission to go theer immadiately. The ould gintleman was thunderstruck—for, do ye mind, she kipt

the real cause a sacret from him—he remon-
strated—pointed out the difficulties of the
undertakin'—its dangers—and, last of all,
his own advanced age, and faable hilth.
But all wud not do. Go she wud; and he
had, from the first, allowed her to have her
own way in iverythin'. He was, therefore,
forced to yield til her intraaties, and furnish
her the necessary funds for the voyage.

"Well, I was sittin' alone in my shop
win day, wid my head laanin' on my hand,
thinkin' of poor Terrence, who was thin
two waaks in his grave, whin the carrier
brought in a litter, post-marked New York,
addressed to Terrence McFarland. My surprise was as if God's lightnin' had claved
the ground undther me, whin, on openin'
and raadin' it, I found it to be from Kate,
who had arrived in that city, and wushed
her brither, of whose death she was ignorant,
to go on and conduct her to Philadilphy!

"Och, but I thought my heart wud milt
wid waapin' afther the raadin' of that litter.
Joy and sorrow, plissure and graif, mingled
thegither, and I that avenin' visited the
Potter's faild in the moonlight, and filt as if

I had a paice of intilligence for my slaipin'
partner theer, which wud be good news til
him aven in his grave. The intinsity of
my graif had enfaabled my undtherstandin'
for the time.

"I wull not attimpt to describe my interview wid my cousin Kate—how we wipt
thegither, and dwilt on the virtues of the
dccaased brither. Pass all that.—Tin
months rolled by, durin' which (as I afther-
ward learned—for she had not informed me
of the circumstance that had induced her to
lave Ireland) she recaived thraa litters from
the ould barristher, urgin' her return, and
tillin' how faable his hilth had become; and
two from the artful cook and her daughther, which abounded wid false accounts of
the scandalous gossip that was circulatin'
fornent her and the barristher aming the
townsfolk.

"At lingth she shewed me a last litter
from the ould gintleman, in which he threat-
ened to cut her off from all bequists in his
will, and to transfare the same til the cook's
daughther, ixcipt she immediately returned.
No sooner had I read this than I saw

through the whole schaam of those wumin at wince.—I blamed her for not havin' lit me intil the sacret before—and urged her return wid all the spaad she could make.

" Mysilf accompanied her ; the voyage to Belfast occupied twinty-nine days ; from thince to the aforemintioned saaport town we weer four days additional, by raason of stage-coach delays. Kate rushed at wince to the barristher's house, and raached his bedside just in time to see him braathe his last !

" Whin the will was read she found hersilf cut aff wid one hundred pounds, and the bulk of the poor decaived old gintleman's fortune was lift til the cook's daughther !

" What thin ? Wull ye suspicion now that Providince favors the guilty, and laaves the virtuous unbefrinded ? Faix, thin, it's a misjudgin' of the justice of Hivven it wud be to conclude so. Kate and I (for ye'll anticipate that we bacame win in holy bonds) niver invied the artful craathers their ill-gotten wilth—nor had we naad. They weer so despised in theer neeborhood,

we afterwards learned, that they weer com-
pilled to remove their risidince to ither parts
wheer they sipposed they wud be unknown.
Theer they sit thimsilves ip for gintlefolk,
but their ignorance and vulgarity of manners betrayed thim for what they weer, and
they soon fell into contimpt and niglict.
This is the last we heard of thim.

"As for Kate and I, we had our tribbles
too; but whin the sunshine of conscience is
not darkened by aavil clouds, all tribbles
may be pretty aasily borne.

"We immadiately returned to Philadilphy, but wid no taste for continuin' in the
business in which her brither and me had
been engaged. I theerfore sold out our
stores of groceries and provisions, and came
hither and bought this paice of ground. It
was naarly all kivered wid traas thin; but
we got it chaap, and my ixparience, whin
a boy, wid the St. Lawrence farmer, had
taught me to claar away wuds pratty
aasily.

"Well, aven these wuds, sparsely popu-
lated as they weer, afforded us new insights
intil human nature; and ispicially did we

16

git lissons on the value of outward profissions of religion, which weer of use til uz.
Paaple in the wuds know each ither mich
better nor do paaple in crowded cities; they
have more daalins wid aach ither, and more
neeborly naad of aach ither's assistance, in
the former nor in the latther.

"It was autumn whin we arrived here,
and we had naad of iverythin' in the way
of provision for the winter, ixcipt a few
articles we brought wid uz of our shop
stores. So I first wint til a Musther Gulphin, who had a large farm and great
abundance of iverythin', and who, besides,
made great pretensions to piety, insomuch
that he praached for the wuds paaple whin
theer rigular praacher did n't serve thim.
In addition to all he was a countrymin of
my own.

"Musther Gulphin," said I, "wull ye
lind a naady neebor a few bushels of rye,
and a few of paraatees, until he raaps his
nixt simmir's harvest, whin he'll repay ye
wid interest?"

"'Indaad I'll do nothin' of the soort,'
said he, 'nothin' but goold can make me

part wid the fruits of my labor. If it's naady of food ye are, sure theer are many ithers like ye, in the world, and it isn't raason that I can hilp thim all.'

"'Do ye hilp *inny* of thim?' I axed; and his only reply was to lave the room in anger and not return til it. So that I was fain to lave also, which I did as impty as I wint.

"My nixt recoorse was til an ould class-laader, who, nixt to Musther Gulphin, was most likely of inny to have the maans of hilpin' me, and, to jidge by his profissions, the wull to do it also. I made the same proposal til him as til the ither. He listened til it wid a gracious smile and said he wud accommodate me. 'But my ter-rms are, in such cases,' said he, 'to require thraa bush-els returned for ivery two I lind, provided the articels be aqually good; and if they are infarior, why I take as mich more as wull make ip the differ.'

"'Faix, thin,' I answered, 'I'll not be likely to tribble ye farder ixcipt it's starvin' I am;' and I returned to my cabin wid a nivvy heart, and a sorry opinion of the

paaple of thase wuds. 'For if the two hist
Christians aming ye are thus could-hearted
and graspin',' thought I, 'what must the
lave of ye be!'

"I had scarcely raached home, howiver,
ere two neebors came til my cabin—and
anither on the same irrand the nixt day—
who offered, of theer own accord, to lind us
iverythin' we wanted in the way of provision, and to take an aqual missure in return
whin my craps should come in. Och, but
it gladded the heart of me to be so agraaibly
undecaived in respict to my neebors, and I
was riddy, at the moment—may God for-
give me if I was wrang!—to ixpriss my
thankfulniss that those wuds contained
some paaple who had not been born again!

"Yes, faix, *who had not been born again;*
for, simhow or anither, it has chanced til me
to find more sympathy and hilp in ivery
time of naad from such, than from those
who profiss to be new craathers in Christ.
and to be in possession of a sure tithel to
hivvenly bliss in a futhur world.

"And yit, my frind, it is not religion that
I wud be scornin' or misdoubtin'; I wud as

soon think of scornin' the right path til my home, because I have mistaken ithers for it ere now and been decaived. As well might I scorn a real rimidy for disase, because sim have been made worse by trustin' til quack nostrums. But in this decaivin' world, my frind, religion is too oftin found lackin in those who profiss to be full of it, and to abound in the timpers and acts of ithers, who, in the world's opinion, are impty of it intirely. Theer is one All-searchin' Eye, which is niver decaived in these matthers; we shud act always wid a riferince to that, and faal contint if its scru-teny of our hearts deticts theer no sintimint, at variance wid our obligations to God and to mankind."

"Eschew invy, 'Tam, as ye wud the devil," said our old friend of the hill-side, "for to spaak Christian trute, and to daal

16*

in honest plainness wid ye, Tam—as my
relationship on yer mither's side warrants
me—I perceive that to that same invy ye
are much inclined, and that it is makin' a
bigger simpleton of ye than ye are by nathur,
which is altogither naadliss."

This was to his nephew, Tom Voodree;
of which name there were two in the parts.
The owner of one lived on a farm by itself
in the midst of the forest, and was therefore
distinguished by the old man as " Tam of
the wuds."   The other owned a grist-mill,
and small bottom-land farm, on a considerable stream in the open country; and was
therefore distinguished from the other by
the cognomen of " Tam of the well."   It is
with him of the mill that the old man is
now having to do.   A hopeful subject he;
who was always very pious when he was
not very drunk; yet, as the community, of
that settlement was almost wholly made up
of his father's family, uncles, aunts, cousins,
&c., who also composed nearly the entire
church in the place, his frequent backslidings were connived at, and he told as good
an experience in the class-meeting as the
best.

"And it's called to be a praacher ye think ye are, Tam! And it's sorely conscience-bound ye are to haad the call, it saams. No doubt ye are. But it's pricious little haad ye've given to the oft-repaated call to forsake yer whesky-bottle, and to attind til yer business, and to pay yer dibts. It's maybe not so plissant a thing, the latter, as to mount yer horse and ride frim place to place, spindin' yer life in rantin' and psalm-singing? Well, Tam, how it may plaise the Loord to rigulate his choice of min for praachers, I pretind not to know; but I know that if I weer the masther of a nimber of servants, and naaded win of thim for an important paice of business, I wud choose for that same win who had proved himsilf faitful in ither matthers in which I had imployed him. Divil a bit wud I be for pickin out win that had always proved himself an idle and unscrupulous fillow. Not a bit of it.

"And, Tam, if it's for a praacher God intended ye, sure its little that nathur could have known of that same whin she made ye, or she wud not have so niglicted the furnishin' of yer upper story—it's naither mitch brain she has given ye, man, nor room for mitch.　True, ye have a big troat, and can cry oysters at naad, or drive oxen, or be a town crier, or the masther of an apple-cart.　But to *praach*, man—Well, whin I bethink me, I don't know but ye maybe have all the qualification ye naad— a big troat will serve ye bether nor a big brain for the paaple wid whom ye'll have to do.　Ye can bawl lustily, Tam, and that will be the chaif of yer naad in yer new capacity."

This dealing with his hopeful nephew was rather *over*-plain, I thought; I like free speech, when it really *is* such and nothing more; but it must not degenerate into abuse, and seek for itself the shelter of a softer name.　I so expressed myself to our old friend as we proceeded together toward his residence, which, from that of " Tam of the well," was distant some three miles or more.　I farther remarked to our blunt old friend, that I feared he had taken up the hackneyed outcry against the Christian ministry in general, which in different ages had so prevailed amongst skeptical scoffers, and demagogues in the cause of reform.

"Maybe I am a bit riffer on my tongue than I faal in my heart," said he, "and, touchin' the praisthood, I maybe faal nin too mitch good-will fornent it; nivertheliss, I am not of thim who denounce it altogither —not by inny maans. Och, but havn't I wipt taars over the story of the Dairyman's Daughther? And havn't I blissed in the heart of me a Haber, and a Finelan, and an Oberlin, who so honored theer profission by doin' the works of their masther aming min? Faix have I.

"But for such genuine ministers of religion, minny is the dyin' pillow that wud go unsmoothed—minny a heart-ach, from graif and beraavement, wud go unhaaled— minny a tinder spirit, overburthened 'wid remorse, wud go uncomforted. In this silfish world, wheer aach of uz is peersuin' his own inds, we naad a class of min for thase spicial offices, in whose bosoms baats the big heart of the Saviour, ful of benivolint yearnins toward the opprissed, the brokenhearted, the frindless, the niglicted by the world, and the like.

"But, on the ither hand; for ful twinty years these wuds have been rigularly visited by praachers; zillous min they have most of thim been; they have kim til uz through thick and thin. But what thin? Do they inquire who of uz are sick?—who beraaved?—who in naad of bread?—who sufferin' wid remorse? What discords require to be haaled? What waak hearts naad bracin' wid the voice of incouragemint? What unsteady son or daughther naads to be stringthined agin' timptation? Och, nothin' of all this. A Paul, plaadin' wid a Philemon, in behalf of a repintent Onisimus, wud be a heart-traat nowadays that wud make uz think that the premitive times of the gospil had kim back til uz.

"And, thin, theer prachin', the main part of it, what relation exists betwaan its topics and man's prissent good? Sorra a ha'porth that I can percaive. They'll ixplain some mysterious tixt, maybe; and the same wul naad re-ixplainin' by the time anither kims along. They'll tache uz who Milchisedic was, and divil the wiser will we be on that head afther all. They'll open the siven saals in Rivelation til uz, and ixplain all its smoke, and brimstone, and locusts, and scorpions, and siven-headed baasts; and whin they are done, all will be as much fog til uz as iver. They'll till us on what terms God will sill his favor til uz; and at the same time will til that his grace is fraa and unpurchased. They'll ripresint the Almighty as all love and goodness, widout variableniss or the shadow of turnin'; and yit till uz that we niver can have his good-will on our side ixcipt we pray, and ago-nize, and faal oursilves to be writches unde-servin' his mercy, and only fit to be burnt in hell; and, afther all, if we can coox him to be pitiful toward uz in the laast, it will be for Jaasus' sake alone, and not at all for ours."

We were now far on our way toward our old friend's residence; we had arrived at a part of the road which runs through a grove of gigantic maples, thinly interspersed with birches and hemlocks, and such continued its character for a quarter of a mile or so.

The road is more broadly cut out there than
it is usual for roads to be in those woods;
yet, from the unfrequency of travel thereon,
it was velvety under foot with the rich pro-
fusion of grass which spontaneously clothed
it; and all the richer in its hue and softness
was that green carpeture, for being shel-
tered from the direct heat of the sun by
those o'ershadowing maples.

It wanted an hour or so of sun-setting,
and the day was one of those in early June
rare in our rigorous clime—when, to everything that lives, mere existence is felt to be
a luxury.   The little birds were either hard
to please with the tunes they tried, or too
heart-full of joy to finish any that they
begun.   The branches of those magnificent
trees met and interlaced overhead, and we
walked as under the vaulted roof of a far-
extending cathedral, or under a lofty colon-
nade of nature's own building.   But neither
under cathedral roofs nor colonnades is it
usual for fountains to gush forth, and squirrels to chirp and exhibit their gymnastics,
as they did under ours.   And the gently-
stirring air was so soft! so freighted with

aroma! It was as if angels were invisibly
fanning our faces with their wings, and
soothing our senses as with odors from
heaven.

We had neither of us broken silence while
passing through this beautiful avenue, nor,
till we had left it far behind us, and were
emerging into the cleared country, did our
old friend, usually so quarrelous, find his
tongue, and he then broke forth in apparent
continuation of where he had last left off. .

"'Procure the favor of God!'. As if it
was a grudge he had agin uz, all the time
that he is smilin' upon uz so plissantly, in
his sun by day, and his moon and stars by
night. Is it decaivin' uz he is, thin, whin
he pours upon uz his sunbaams, and sprids,
as he does now, the cloudliss face of hivven
over uz? And are we to doubt him all the
while that he is spaakin' the music of paace
til the heart, in the voices of birds, and
brooklets, and murmurin' braazes, which
so tranquillize the spirit whin it is riffled
wid the stormy passions and competitions
of silfish life? Och, but it's not myself
that can misdoubt all thase claar tokens.

17

I could sooner renounce belaif in inny and iverythin' man has written, and aven in the printed documents of our religion thimsilves. For the last may have kim til uz wid minny corruptions and false rinderins; but God's unprinted book is frishly opened til uz ivery night and mornin'; and we naad no note nor commint to hilp uz undtherstand, that, in spite of all our undeservins, it's still our faitful and unchanging frind the Author of that blissed volume foriver continues to be."

The cleared country of which I spoke comprises ten or a dozen farms, of which the old man's is one; the latter is on the outer edge of the clearing, and is bounded by an extensive tract of wilderness, which is unaltered from its primeval state, save by dimly-discernible foot-prints, and by slight abrasions on here and there the bark of a tree, as a means of guidance to those who have need of traversing it. The sun had entirely set,

> ———" And twilight gray
> Had in her sober livery all things clad," ·

as we passed the copse of chestnuts which

overshadow Terrence McFarland's grave.
I noticed that the old man—but with the
least possible ostentation, mind you, for
such was his character—walked with head
uncovered past that sacred spot, and as
reverently as would a Catholic past the
shrine of a saint.

Arrived at the cabin, Kate received us
with a welcoming smile, and placed a chair
for each of us, which she dusted off with
her apron; not that it stood in any such
need, but to gratify the desire natural to a
loving heart, to be constantly doing something for somebody. We had eaten our
supper, and were seated, for coolness' sake,
on a small piece of grassy sward before the
door, when the old man (who, I found,
was much given to reverie) again broke out
on the theme which had last engaged our
conversation, and with as much abruptness
as though nothing had intervened meanwhile.

"No, indaad," said he, "man may make
a foe of himsilf—he may sink himsilf in his
own just estaam—but his God is still, and
unchangeably, love toward him. Con-

science lies coiled widin him like a rattle-snake—harmliss till thrampled on—whin he approaches forbidden limits she gives her premonitory rattle; if that is not haaded, and he procaads to ixccute his avil designs, she thin darts her vinemous fang intil his soul, and a foul disaase is transfused troo-out the same which nothin' but hivvenl· grace can counteract.

"Frim hincefort his own avil shadde stands iver betwaan God and his perciptions—he jidges of his Maker by himsilf—as if the brightniss of the sun could be jidged of by lookin' at it troo a paice of smoked glass—he imputes to the Daity his own anger, jillousy, revingefulniss, mutability, waakniss, favooritcism, and iverything of the soort; and his craad is shaped accordingly. Listen til what the craad taaches, and ye'll belaive that Hivven is betther plaised wid thim that can raad riddles, and yaild an aasy cradince to whativer is pit down til thim frim the pulpit, than wid thim who love to be useful and benivolent. The former are the wins that are to shine brightest in the firmamint afther ·they are dead. And, faix, they ought to shine *sim-wheer*, for little is the light the most of thim have shid on earth.

"Since we have lived in thase wuds, Kate and I have communed mitch on thase subjects; we ask no minister's laave to think as we plaase fornint thim, and we have long since caased to belaave the child-ish fancy, that the Daity missures out his goodwill toward his rational offspring by the amount of their credulity. In thase thinly paapled wuds we injoy our opinions in quiet; and whin we go hince, our trust is in God's mercy that our bodies will rist nin the liss quietly theer for unther the chisnut copse, nor our spirits be liss paace-ful in the bosom of him who gave thim.

"This, frind, is more of the ould man's craad than he has iver gratified human curi-osity wid before. Lit uz up and intil the housc, for the avenin' dews are descindin' on uz more plintifully than will be for our hilth."

17*

www.ingramcontent.com/pod-product-compliance
Lightning Source LLC
Chambersburg PA
CBHW030551040726
47497CB00008B/2678